TRACE TAKES A HAND

Years ago, the Arista gang stole fifty thousand dollars — only for one member to escape with the whole haul ... The traitor, Luke Cason, is living quietly with his daughter Sally — until he is abducted by his former associates, seeking both vengeance and the money. Meanwhile, Texas state marshal Trace Cavanagh is staking plenty on a big gamble: taking two convicts from the penitentiary to assist him in hunting the gang. When their path crosses with Sally's, lawkeepers and lawbreakers alike must join forces to track down the deadly Aristas ...

OWEN G. IRONS

TRACE TAKES A HAND

Complete and Unabridged

LINFORD
Leicester

First published in Great Britain in 2013 by
Robert Hale Limited
London

First Linford Edition
published 2015
by arrangement with
Robert Hale Limited
London

A catalogue record for this book is available
from the British Library.

ISBN 978–1–4448–2610–4

Published by
F. A. Thorpe (Publishing)
Anstey, Leicestershire

Set by Words & Graphics Ltd.
Anstey, Leicestershire
Printed and bound in Great Britain by
T. J. International Ltd., Padstow, Cornwall

This book is printed on acid-free paper

1

The summer had been hot across the west Texas plains. When Luke Cason first saw the strange riders approaching his small Independence ranch which lay along the Pecos River, they appeared like dark wraiths riding through a heat haze. Luke squinted into the sun and reached up on to the porch of his white clapboard house with the green roof for his Winchester '73. Luke was a friendly man but not a trusting one. Not after the life he had led.

In the doorway of the house stood Sally Cason, wearing a light blue dress and a white apron. The young woman brushed back a strand of hair from her forehead with the back of her wrist. Her eyes shifted in the direction her father was looking.

'Who is it?' she asked, shading her eyes with her hand.

'I don't know,' Luke Cason answered. 'Maybe just men passing by. Maybe . . . go back into the house, Sally, and down into the basement.'

'The basement?' Sally said in surprise. The cellar was reached via a trapdoor in the kitchen floor. Sally almost never went down there. She remembered only vaguely the early years on the ranch when the Comanches had still been a threat, that she and her mother had gone down there to hide during a brief skirmish in which no one was killed, but an old ranch hand named Tate was seriously wounded.

'Yes. Do as I say!'

Confused, Sally complied dutifully. Rushing across the house, she went into the kitchen, tossing her apron on to the counter as she went. Then she opened the grudging trap door and slipped down into the cobwebbed, musty cellar, letting the heavy door close behind her. She locked it firmly with the barrel lock fastened there, sank into the dark, silent corner of the room and waited for what was to come.

Luke Cason continued to stand in front of his porch, his rifle at the ready. Still through the heat veils he could not make out the faces of the riders, but he knew who they had to be — old sins are never forgotten. The line of dark, distorted figures were approaching him from his past and they had come to demand payment. Luke continued to hold his fire. There was a chance that he could be wrong, and he did not wish to start a gunfight with Sally in the house. He thought there would be little choice in the matter.

Sally Cason could see little in the darkened cellar; she could hear little. The sounds from outside were muffled by the thick walls and heavy trapdoor. She strained eyes and ears. She got to her feet as she heard what she took for sharp rapping on the front door of the house. Why would they be knocking at the door with her father outside? Shivering now with the coolness of the cellar and with the fear which had begun to sink into her heart, she recognized the sounds for what they were.

The rapid pelting sounds were muffled gunshots. There were many of them. A dozen, twenty. Then they fell away leaving a dark and gloomy silence.

Bootheels sounded against the floorboards above Sally's hiding place. Someone spoke in a deep tone. No one answered. Sally lifted her eyes toward the trap door, hoping, praying that it would swing open to reveal light and the sturdy face of her father.

It did not.

A voice spoke again, uttering a few indistinguishable words, then the boots walked away, shaking the floor just enough to send light dust sifting down into the cellar. Sally withdrew into the far corner and cringed there, waiting and watching, her heart beating wildly. She hoped for the best, but feared the worst. The hardest part of it all, to her, was not being able to see what was happening, to help if help was needed. She made a silent vow to never hide again from trouble when it came visiting.

Long minutes passed, hours? She thought she heard horses being walked away, but could not be sure. There was only the darkness, the silence, the musty smell of the cellar. She suppressed a momentary urge to shriek out her frustration. She stood, fists clenched, her eyes futilely searching the darkness, her hearing alert for sounds which never came.

Her senses seemed useless in the depths of this small dark chamber. Then her head came up sharply and she was spurred into motion. Her senses had not proved futile, only those she had been depending on.

Smoke.

She could smell it quite clearly — the scent of cured lumber burning. The house had been set afire.

With a muffled gasp and with instant decision, Sally scrambled toward the ladder leading up into the house, fumbling with her skirts as she climbed. Smoke curled into the cellar the instant the trapdoor was thrown back. Sally knew that there was a basin of water and a washcloth still out on the counter. She had been preparing to wash the breakfast dishes. Now she staggered that way and soaked the washcloth, holding it over mouth and nostrils as she made her unsteady way toward the door.

Smoke in the outer room was much heavier, scented with coal oil. Sally had to feel her way along the wall which was heated. Her eyes smarted from the smoke which seemed to lower like a falling curtain across the room. Beyond, in her bedroom, she could now see live flames licking at the walls and curling up toward the ceiling. She did not try to make her way there to retrieve her few possessions.

Her only thoughts were on her own survival — and that of her father. She would have expected Luke Cason to have rushed to the cellar or at least have cried out to her if he were able. Something seemed to reignite the dying flames. Perhaps they had touched another pool of coal oil. The fire suddenly flared up in front of her and the entire house seemed to be engulfed. Had she remained in the cellar she would have been trapped, suffocating slowly to death by now. As it was she was near enough to the door to see a way out, open land beyond.

Ribbons of bright flame hung from the eaves of the porch like scarlet garlands; the uprights were blackened and eaten away, appearing like huge matchsticks. Sally needed no one to tell her they were unstable.

As was the entire roof. Now, as she lurched toward the door, the ceiling opened up and sections of roof beams followed by tumbling shingles caved inward. The flames inside the house leaped skyward as if attracted by the oxygen, and the entire house became a conflagration.

Barely able to breathe despite having her mouth covered with the washcloth, Sally raced toward the front door, tripping over a burning fallen timber. She breached the doorway in time to watch the curling flames do their final damage to the porch awning and it began to sag badly at one end. Sally leaped clumsily into the yard as the house and the attached structure, sagged, spewed black smoke and gave up its battle against the fire.

The roof caved in, scarlet flames jutted high, smoke curled and roiled in the wind. Platter-sized pieces of ash sailed upward and then settled. Sally kept moving, away from the intense heat and strangling black smoke. She threw away the washcloth which now steamed against her face. A hundred feet from the house she stopped in the shade of the three cottonwood trees growing there, bending over at the waist, breathing in deeply. The heat of the fire was still intense against her body, on her face. Her ankles felt singed, and looking down she saw that the hem of her skirt had been touched by fire. Using her hands she slapped out these tiny remnants of the flames within the house and stood in the scant shade of the trees, watching as her home slowly buckled and collapsed.

When it hit the ground it made a terrific sound, like a cannon's roar. The flames that had been tall, flicking at the belly of the pale sky now began to dwindle. But still the black smoke rose heavily, a swarm of small tongues of fires ate at the remains of the house.

Where was her father? She knew that he could not be alive; he would have never left her where she was if he could have done a single thing to prevent it.

Sally stood with her hands to her cheeks searching the area with her eyes. An odd smell reached her nostrils, and she realized that her hair was singed. Slapping angrily at her skull, she reflected both on how long she had taken dressing her hair that morning and how unimportant it was now.

She was a woman alone in an empty, depleted world where black smoke hovered low across the earth and ever so slowly dissipated with the wind. Hell fire had dwindled to bright, angry memories. Her father was gone. There was no point in watching the remains of the house, the fire burning itself out, and so she started a slow survey of the yard. The barn was empty; the three horses had scattered in fright. The yellow grass stubble was blackened from the heat.

The pale high sky remained featureless. Heat shimmers still rose from the long white flats toward the Pecos River. Not a bird stirred, no small animals fled before her boots. The fire had scattered them all, frightened them away.

She could see no trace of her father. Her worst fear was that the raiders — whoever they had been — had gunned Luke Cason down, but that did not seem to be the case. Why would they take the body with them? No, her father was alive, but wounded? They had taken him away with them, and it would not be to seek treatment for him.

Why, then?

Who would ride into this barren, lost country to find her father, and then, having found him, ridden away with him? Would he ever be able to free himself and make his way back? Giving up her search, Sally Cason seated herself on the fallen trunk of a cottonwood tree and stared blankly into the distances, away from the ruin of a house which still smoldered in its death, and took stock.

She was alone, completely alone. She was afoot: the horses had run off or been taken. The nearest town of any sort was Sheffield and that lay almost seventy miles to the south. They had no neighbors, something that her father had appreciated although it had made for a lonely childhood for Sally.

She sniffed and reached for a handkerchief in her skirt pocket. She was about to cry — and darnit! — she did not want to cry. Her eyes were still smoke-irritated. There was a hitch in her breathing from inhaling some of the stuff. Her skirt had a funny scorched ring around it. Her house, the only home she could remember ever having lay in a dry puddle of ash and destruction.

She was an orphan — or as good as — alone on the long, dry, west Texas plains. Her only relative, her only friend — her father — had apparently been spirited away unless he was hiding somewhere, and that seemed unlikely. She raised her hands skyward in a gesture of futility and then decided:

Well, darnit, I have the right to cry! And she did.

After half an hour or so of feeling sorry for herself, Sally gave one last snuffle and rose to her feet. She had to do something to help herself, but what was there to do? The house lay almost flat against the earth, still smoldering. The white sun rode high against the pale sky, shafting beams of light through the dark smoke which hovered over the ruins of the building.

Sally had no horse, no food, no water and nowhere to go. Her shelter, safety and security had all turned to ashes. Water — that was the first thing. She knew there was at least one old canteen hanging in the barn. She would fill that and walk, walk as far away as she could. It was best to leave ruined memories behind as quickly as possible.

If she followed the Pecos River southward she would always have a source of water, and there was the chance she might be able to hail one of the occasional flatboats which plied the river, hauling furs and buffalo hides nearer to the trading routes, though these boats were not as plentiful as they once had been with the buffalo die-off.

No matter. It was a chance, and Sally had made up her mind that she had to move. She only wished that her jeans, coat and sturdy boots could be rescued from the ashes, but she knew that was not possible. The burnt heap of wood still breathed heat. Even after the ashes had cooled it was unlikely that any of these items could be found or had survived in usable condition.

Well, her father had always said: 'We have to work with what we've got, not with what we wish we had.' What Sally had was very little indeed. She circled once more toward the barn, carrying a vague hope that one of the horses, frightened away by the fire might have returned. It was a futile hope. The barn remained empty. It was hot inside, nearly as hot as it had been in the burning house itself.

She found a half-gallon canteen hanging on its canvas strap from a nail driven into the wall and unhooked it. Putting the strap over her shoulder she hiked back through the drifting smoke and the heat toward the well. Some small component of the house snapped and collapsed, startling her. She felt that she had to get away from this small corner of hell as rapidly as possible now that she had decided that there was no choice but to leave.

The heat of the day burned her feet through the thin leather of her house shoes. She caught a glimpse of a black-tailed jack rabbit — the first living thing she had seen since the fire. It sat panting in the shade of the cottonwood trees. Twitching one upright ear toward her, it loped away with apparent lethargy.

The rope to the well bucket had not been touched by fire. Sally tugged up the bucket and started to drink from it. But there was a layer of ash on its surface. She skimmed it off angrily. There was ash dust on everything. Her hands were black with the stuff, her clothes, the new grass . . . she paused to take a deep breath, stilling her anger at things that could not be helped. After two attempts she managed to fill her canteen. There was no telling what the formerly sweet water might taste like, but it was key to her survival.

She rested for a moment, leaning against the hot wooden box of the well cap. For a moment she stood watching the strange dark curlicues sketched by the smoke against the sky in the shifting breeze. There was something eerily fascinating about their movements.

This was doing her no good! Pulling herself erect, shouldering the canteen, Sally walked through the heated shade of the cottonwood trees and started her desperate journey eastward toward the Pecos.

She trudged across the white, empty land toward the river, its cooling influence only a distant longing. On the flats all was still, barren and sere. She tried singing to cheer herself, but found her throat was dry and her lungs were still stained with ash dust.

Plodding on across the limitless land, she then tried to imagine what her future life would be like. She dreamed in a fantastic way of satins, silk and fine jewelry before deciding that she would be appreciative of a home, safety, food and cool water — lots of cool water.

Well, once she reached the river, there was a chance at least, and once she arrived in some town — any nondescript frontier town — she was bound to be better off than she was now. Because at this moment, Sally was sure that things could not get any worse.

And then they did.

She saw them riding in a line. Three men, their figures elongated by the rising heat veils, their figures black and ominous, shimmering, but all too solid.

They had come back!

Sally halted and watched the riders who seemed to be emerging from pale smoke. Where her thoughts had been desperate, they now turned to heated anger. Where she had wished for a horse, sturdy boots and jeans, she now only wished that she had a gun in her hands to deliver bloody justice to the dark riders.

2

'There's someone,' Raven said, rising in his stirrups, pointing westward.

'I see her,' Trace Cavanaugh answered with a nod. His voice was toneless. The tall man with the deeply tanned face and ice-blue eyes halted his big gray horse.

'She's just standing there,' Woody Price, by far the youngest of the three, said with concern. He removed his Stetson briefly to mop his brow with his red kerchief. His straw-yellow hair tumbled out and he wiped it back. There was concern on his boyish face.

It was true, the slight woman they had come upon was simply standing there across the white flats, staring at them.

'That's about all she can do,' Trace said. 'Can't run away from us, hide.'

'Maybe she's in shock,' Raven said,

leaning forward in his saddle. His dark eyes were intent.

Black smoke still curled skyward in the distance, twisting in the wind. Something bad had happened here, that was certain. And the girl must have been a part of it, or witness to it. There was no other place she could be coming from.

'We'd better talk to her,' Raven said, stroking his thick black mustache. Trace nodded again.

'If she's not out of her mind she should be able to tell us something.'

And she could well be out of her mind if she had witnessed mayhem, murder and had been wandering around hatless in the blazing heat of the sun. She did resemble survivors of an Indian attack Trace had found on the plains after their wagon train had been attacked. Those people, men and women, seemed to have been driven half-crazy by events and deprivation. Trace started his horse forward, Raven and Woody Price falling in behind him.

They approached the woman who continued to stand staring at them. There was fire in her eyes, the sort of look one did not see in a person who had, defeated, allowed herself to sink into madness.

Sally Cason watched the riders approaching her through the heat glare of the day and the wisps of dark smoke which had somehow drifted this far from the burned house. She waited for them to make their slow arrival. There was nothing else to do. There was nowhere to flee. She had already decided that defiance would be her best defense and she stood ready to deliver her defiant word as the man on the gray horse halted a few yards from her and the others flanked him.

'If you want me, you'll have a fight on your hands!' Sally said as loudly as her smoke-damaged voice could manage. She knew there was soot on her face, that her dress was scorched and smudged and that her hair had been singed. She must have looked like some sort of wild woman, but maybe that was all for the good. It might give them pause to think. She glared at them, hands on hips and waited for what might come next. When their reply did come, it was nothing like she had expected.

'Fine,' Trace said without inflection, 'but I don't want you. Raven, do you want her?'

'Not me. She's too young and a little too scrawny for me.' This man, the one with the heavy black mustache was smiling, and it irritated Sally unreasonably. Raven went on, 'Maybe Woody would want her. He's a bit younger than we are. What about it, Woody?'

The boy obviously did not wish to be drawn into the bantering. His face flushed beneath its tan. 'Ah! I don't know what you two are talking about, but it seems the woman is in need of some help.'

'I need nothing from you!' Sally said in rebuke, 'nor would I expect any from a pack of animals such as you!'

21

Woody flushed again — what had he said that was so wrong? Raven had tipped back his black hat with the silver band; his smile had not faded.

'What are you going to do, girl? Walk to the Pecos? Try floating down it?'

That angered Sally even more, for that was very near the plan she had in mind.

'What happened over there?' Trace asked Sally, nodding toward the rising smoke. 'Comanches?' Trace and everyone else knew that outside of an occasional reservation jumper, Comanches had not been seen in the area for years. Woody knew that as well, and he glanced at Trace Cavanaugh, wondering what had prompted him to make such a suggestion.

'You know it wasn't Comanches!' Sally spat back. 'It was you who did it.'

'You're wrong there, girl,' Raven said. 'We're looking for a man named Cason. Luke Cason. We considered that this was his ranch.'

'We're friends of Luke's,' Trace said,

seeing the tangle of emotions behind the girl's eyes.

'Then what did you do with him! Why did you take him away?' Sally demanded, her hands curling into tight fists.

'Not us,' Raven said. He looked at Woody and smiled. 'The girl thinks we want to take everybody away. I wonder where we'll put them all?'

Trace took over, speaking calmly and quietly. 'Look,' he said to Sally, 'it's true there aren't many men riding across this country, but you must be mistaking us for some other men. I think I know who they were, and it's no coincidence that they came to the house just before us. We've been trailing after those four for many miles. There were four of them, weren't there?'

'I don't know. I can't be sure,' Sally had to tell him. 'Father told me to hide in the cellar, and I did. I stayed there until the fire started burning.'

'You're Luke Cason's daughter?'

Raven asked, raising one eyebrow. Sally nodded.

'And you say that Luke . . . your father was taken away by these men?' Trace asked.

'He has to have been. I couldn't find him, not even his . . . they have to have taken him, but I can't imagine why.'

'So they never even saw you?' Raven asked.

'No,' Sally replied. She was still uncertain about the three men facing her. The big gray horse shuffled its feet and blew through its nostrils. 'I thought you were those men — I never saw them either.'

Raven was still in one of his whimsical moods. Grinning, he asked Sally, 'So you thought we took your father away and then came back to take him again?'

Having it put that way made Sally Cason aware of how foolish her assumption sounded to them. But she had thought . . . 'What can we do now?' she asked sincerely, speaking to the tall man on the gray horse.

'Should we go over to the house and take a look around?' the youngest member of the trio, Woody Price asked.

'I don't imagine there's much to see, little to be learned,' Trace answered. He looked at Sally who shook her head dismally.

'A pile of burnt rubble and dead ash,' she said. 'But you could pick up their sign, couldn't you,' Sally asked hopefully, 'and ride them down? I know they have my father.'

Raven told her, 'These are experienced trailsmen; they know full well how to cover their tracks. Trace?'

Cavanaugh had been listening, briefly meditating. He sighed now and straightened in his saddle, looking toward the south. 'No, I think we're better off striking out toward the river. They'll have to follow it for water. They can't know this country well enough to rely on springs and seasonal streams.'

He added, to Sally, 'We'll find these men. It may take a while, but we will find them, and free Luke Cason if he is indeed their prisoner.'

'Of course he is! He wouldn't go willingly, leaving me behind out here.'

'But you didn't see what happened, did you?' Raven asked a little cynically. Sally glared at him.

'I didn't have to see it to know my father wouldn't desert me,' she said strongly.

'Could he have been trying to lead them away from his daughter?' Woody chipped in.

'We won't know until we find him,' Trace said. 'And we will find Luke Cason. Come on, girl, you'll have to ride along at least as far as the Pecos.'

'Not behind me,' Raven said, patting his neat little black pony with three white stockings and a white blaze on its nose. 'Dante doesn't like carrying double.'

Trace said, 'You mean you don't want a woman riding behind you.' He was right, but Raven wasn't about to admit it.

'That's not true, Trace,' he wagged his head with mock disappointment in his friend. 'You know I always speak highly of women. Am I not the first to admit that they do have their uses?'

Trace refused to be drawn in to any more of Raven's verbal raillery. 'Girl . . . '

Sally felt offended. There was no reason for it except that her nerves were worn thin. 'I'm a woman, not a girl,' she said, 'and my name is Sally, Sally Cason.'

Raven smiled, feeling vindicated in his decision. He did not like feisty women, and had a near-dread of furious ones. As he had said, he liked them well enough, and they did have their uses — but one of them was not mounting behind him and troubling Dante. Besides that, he had the feeling that she would want to talk to him sooner or later along the trail. Another thing he did not like about women was the way they scattered and drove their conversation.

'Sally,' Trace Cavanaugh said with patience, realizing the girl had been through hell on this heated day, 'you can ride up behind Woody Price here at least until we reach the Pecos River.'

Unaccountably, Woody began again to blush furiously. Raven let out a laugh and turned his black pony southward as Sally, assisted by Woody Price, mounted behind the young man on his stocky buckskin horse.

They trailed on, white dust rising from their horses' hoofs. Soon there was no black smoke to be seen against the sky and the sun had begun to lower its head wearily in the west. Raven rode beside Trace; behind them on the buckskin was Woody Price, unnaturally stiff in his saddle, the girl behind him, not clinging, but keeping her hands on his waist for reassurance.

'The kid looks nervous,' Raven said.

'You could have saved him that,' Trace answered without turning his head.

'Yeah, but you know me, Trace. I only

like women when they have their perfume and silks on. Besides,' he said reflectively, 'maybe it'll do the kid some good as far as growing up.'

'That's thoughtful of you,' Trace answered.

'Yeah,' Raven drawled, knowing Trace was gibing. 'I sure hope we find that river soon. I can hardly stand the thought of another dry camp.'

'You know this part of the country better that I do,' Trace told him.

'Yeah, but it never seems the same, Trace. Like it changes from time to time just to lose a man.'

The white land was beginning to flush with the red of the dying sun before they saw a hopeful indication of water. Trace lifted a pointing finger and Raven nodded his reply. Ahead now they could make out a narrow, curved strip of gray-green. That would be plant growth along a watercourse, and the watercourse had to be the Pecos River. Cresting a low rise they allowed the horses to rest for a minute. From there

Trace could see the band of the river, pewter-silver in this light and a long line of willow brush and sycamore trees fronting the water. The Pecos was shallow and narrow at this time of year, and they saw no sign of flatboat men or their rafts.

And no sign of the Arista gang and their assumed prisoner, Luke Cason. Raven removed his hat and wiped back his gray-streaked black hair. He spoke to Trace as they waited for the buckskin carrying Woody and Sally Cason to join them. The horse, carrying double, had chosen to lag, probably to show its displeasure at being forced to carry extra weight.

'I heard the girl talking, Trace. She was telling Woody that she heard at least a dozen shots before the ranch was torched.' Trace glanced at Raven, his eyes asking the question. 'So, why,' Raven went on, 'was Cason shooting at them if he meant to go along?'

'He didn't mean to go along,' Trace believed. 'The girl's right: Luke was kidnapped. He was trying to fight them off, but then he realized there was no way he was going to win. He went along with their demands to protect his daughter from — '

'From what she has right now,' Raven said.

'He couldn't have known they'd set fire to his home.'

'Why did they?'

'So he couldn't simply slip away and go home. That's the way Regal Arista thinks. Give a man no option and he's likely to be more compliant.' Raven, who did not know Trace's last-used word, shrugged and thought it over.

'He saw what they were about, and he knew his daughter was still inside the house. Why didn't he stop them?'

'He'd already surrendered his weapon by then. It must have been hell for him, but there was nothing he could do. He still couldn't let them find Sally. He must have only hoped that the cellar would protect her from the flames.'

'That was a risk!' Raven said. 'If he had stopped them they would have brought Sally out to ride with them.'

'That was the one thing he couldn't allow,' Trace replied. 'If they had his daughter, there was no way he could escape them. They would have Sally held hostage to use against him.'

'I suppose,' Raven said dourly. 'Well, I never did like Regal Arista. I sure wouldn't want my daughter riding with him . . . had I a daughter.'

'No. Do you see anyone out there?' Trace asked, indicating the dry land and the long stretch of the river with one sweeping gesture.

'No. Do you think we're close to catching up with them?'

'I don't know,' Trace answered. 'I just don't want them catching up with us.'

Raven shifted in the saddle and looked out across the shadowed land behind them. Trace was right. It had been a long day of slow travel across a vast land, but who knew if they were now behind or ahead of the Arista bunch? The gang's lead had been cut by their travel to and back from the Cason ranch. They could now be anywhere out there.

One thing seemed certain: all trails led to the river below them and, as Woody and Sally reached them, they started down the long slope toward the Pecos.

* * *

It was quiet, cool as dusk settled on the Pecos River. There were tall cattails in profusion, marsh grass, willow brush, cottonwood trees and scattered sycamores all clustered around the source of their life — the river. There was a path along the bank leading southward, and after searching in the dim light for tell-tale signs of other horses having passed, Trace led the riders on, searching for a spot to make night camp.

They found a sheltered clearing not much farther along. Sparse grass grew there and the path to the river was clear of brush and reeds. Cottonwood trees clustered near, sheltering them, casting faint shadows which trembled against the earth as an evening breeze rose. All was calm, peaceful.

Sally Cason could be heard to murmur with pleasure as she slipped from the back of the horse to stretch and breathe in the cool evening air. Earlier they had had thick swarms of gnats hovering about them, but now they had died down, although mosquitoes had taken their place in the ranks of annoyance. The ground was soft; sandy but not damp.

'Will you see to my horse for me, Woody?' Trace asked as he swung his saddle heavily from the gray's back.

'Yes, sir,' Sally heard the boy say. It was almost as if Woody were eager to be away from her, and she did not understand. After a little while as she rode behind Woody on the trail she had struck up a conversation with the blond kid, and he had responded with what she had taken as warmth. He spoke shyly, to be sure, but seemed to listen to her with interest. After a while he no longer held himself so rigidly upright in the saddle and seemed not to object to her occasional looping of her arms around his waist when they traversed a rough section of trail, which she appreciated because gripping the cantle of the saddle provided little in the way of security.

Woody Price was Sally's own age or near it. He was probably a few years older, she decided. He had handsomeness about him, though it was not of the classical sort. His ears were not even, she concluded, after spending hours behind him on the horse, studying them. He was soft-spoken, polite and apparently rugged enough to be riding with these two men. But she did not really know him, had nothing to judge him by.

Nor, she realized, did she know either of the other two men whom she had been convinced to ride with. There was something vaguely disturbing about the one they called Raven. His smile, when it came, was a twitch of the lips beneath that drooping heavy mustache. His eyes were black and gave no indication of what he was thinking. She had been given to understand that he had had problems with women in his past.

Trace Cavanaugh was even more enigmatic. What was he? Who was he? He seemed to be in charge, but where did his authority come from? The tall man with the deeply tanned face and firm expression, reminded her in some indefinable way of her father. Probably it was just that they were both western pioneers cut from the same rugged bolt of cloth.

Trace Cavanaugh was spreading out his bedroll on the ground. He had started a small fire with dead wood collected from beneath the sycamore trees and it now burned pleasantly in the center of the clearing, brightening the darkness, driving the worst of the swarming mosquitoes away.

From his pack Chase had dragged out a coffee pot and ground coffee beans and was now boiling coffee. The scent was aromatic and pleasant. Sally watched him hunkered over the fire. The two other men were down at the river, watering their horses. She decided to ask him a few questions. What could it hurt? The worst he could do was refuse to answer.

If she was going to be traveling the wilderness trail with three men she had just met, Sally decided that she had the right to at least know something about her companions. She opened her mouth to approach the subject when Trace suddenly got to his feet and turned her way.

'I don't want you to be frightened by anything I might tell you, Sally, but you have to be made aware that you now find yourself in the company of dangerous men.'

3

After Trace's comment, Sally sat staring up at the tall man for a long silent moment. Her voice, still smoke-dry and desert parched, managed to squeak out the question, 'What do you mean?'

'I shouldn't have said a thing at all,' Trace answered, as he poked at the fire and shifted the coffee pot to one side. He lifted his eyes to the dark river. 'As long as they're taking a while, I thought you should know a few things, seeing as you're traveling with us. After you've heard what I have to say, you can leave of course.' He turned his gaze toward the river again.

'But you wouldn't recommend it?' Sally asked shakily as Trace poured her a tin cup of full of hot black coffee.

'No,' Trace said seriously. 'I think you need our help to find your father — and our protection out here.'

'I suppose I do,' Sally admitted, touching her lips to the coffee; finding it was still too hot to consider drinking. 'Why tell me anything at all?'

'Because you might get to thinking things over and come to all of the wrong conclusions. A man might drop a word here and there and you might take it wrong. Our minds are where we develop our reality. I thought I would give you a few facts so that you'd be able to draw honest conclusions.'

'You're a Texas Ranger, aren't you?' Sally asked out of nowhere.

'No. I'm a Texas State Marshal,' Trace replied, sipping his own coffee.

'Well, the same thing.'

Trace nodded soberly. 'Except that we have different organizations and different responsibilities,' he told her. Was he teasing her?

'Not the same,' she murmured.

'Only in that we all carry badges.' With a sigh, as if it was necessary to prove something to the girl, he reached in an inside breast pocket and removed a badge, showing it briefly to her.

'Why don't you wear it?' she enquired.

'It makes too good a target.'

Sally was briefly thoughtful, sipping at her coffee. 'What about them?' she asked, inclining her head toward the river.

'Them? No, miss, they're not lawmen, but convicts.'

'Men you've arrested?' Sally asked in a tight voice.

'No. Men I've had released,' Trace said, puzzling Sally more. 'They're out of prison on my personal bond. If they fulfil the work I've asked them to do, they will probably be released for good behavior.'

'What if they turn on you? Kill you and make their own way?' asked Sally, slightly terrified.

'Things would only get worse for them then. Killing a state officer is a lot more serious than what they were arrested for. They'd be hanged if they were ever found. Besides,' Trace said with a rare smile, 'the boys and I get along. They know I've helped them and now they only want to do what's right and earn their release.'

'I don't understand,' Sally said. 'Why would you take two convicts out of prison instead of using your own deputies?'

'Raven was a member of the Arista gang for years,' Trace replied, again lifting his eyes toward the sinuous dark river. 'He knows how they think and how they go about their business. Raven is the one who told me that he knew where they were riding — to find Luke Cason.'

'But why?' Sally wanted to know. None of it made sense to her. 'Why my father?'

Trace was hesitant, but he had decided to tell Sally what he thought she needed to know. 'Luke Cason was a member of the Arista gang, according to Raven.'

'He can't have been!' Sally exclaimed. 'Raven must have lied to you.'

'Do you think so? After what has happened?'

'But my father . . . ' She shook her head. 'He was always home — working hard.'

'This was quite awhile ago, Sally. He was riding with the Arista gang. He wanted to get out — for you, likely — and that was why he found a place so far out in this empty country. He knew they would come looking for him one day.'

'But why?'

'Raven says that Luke had something they wanted.'

'Raven says!' Sally sparked up. 'Maybe Raven is a big liar, have you thought of that? Using you to get his release from prison?'

'No,' Trace said calmly. 'I never thought that. I've known Raven for many years.'

Not to be sidetracked, Sally kept on, 'Raven! What kind of name is that anyway? Probably made that up as well.'

'He did that,' Trace admitted to her.

'He is of Italian stock. He was christened Bartolio d'Ravenna. Long ago he decided that was too much name to carry around.'

Sally looked defeated. Trace believed everything he said, that was obvious. Everything he had been told. Sally could not.

'What is it my father was supposed to have that Arista wanted so bad?'

'Fifty-thousand dollars in gold,' Trace told her without changing his expression. Sally's face fell. She began to laugh, to grow angry, and then found equanimity. 'That's absurd.'

'Is it? It's supposed to be in a bank deposit box in Sheffield. Money that was taken from the gang by your father.'

'According to Raven!'

'According to Raven, who was there at the time.'

Sally shifted, leaning forward on her knees. 'We never had any money, Mr Cavanaugh. My father scraped just to get by.'

'Did you ever go to Sheffield, Sally?'

'Hardly ever. It's over seventy miles away, as you know. Once a year at Christmastime we'd go there and Father would buy me a few presents.'

'After stopping at the bank.'

'Yes,' Sally said almost inaudibly. One other seemingly inconsequential thing had occurred to her: her father had worn a small brass key on a chain around his neck. She had asked what it was for, but had never gotten an answer. Now she asked Trace, 'Those safety deposit boxes — do you need a key to get in?'

'A key and the box number — you can't just walk in with a key and start trying it in each box, trying to find which one it might fit.'

'So they couldn't have just taken the key — if they could find it. They needed to take my father . . . or obtain the box number, which he wouldn't have given up easily.' Sally said, a quiet sort of resignation settling over her. She still did not believe that her father had been an outlaw, a thief, but . . .

'Was Raven arrested for being with the Arista gang?' she asked.

'No, he had apparently already quit Regal Arista over some dispute or other. He was arrested in San Antonio for killing a woman.'

Sally's mind whirled, remembering certain statements Raven had made, statements indicating that he had had trouble with women in his life. 'He killed a woman!' The crime was virtually unheard of on the Texas plains or anywhere else in the West for that matter.

'Sort of,' Trace said enigmatically. 'The woman is dead and Raven caused it, legally.'

'I don't understand you,' Sally said, offering her coffee cup for a refill. Trace poured it for her and then was silent for a long while. Finally he seemed to decide that since he had gone this far in divulging confidential information, he might as well go all the way.

'Raven got into a fight with a woman — her name was Emma Goodwine.

They were in his upstairs room in the Soiree Hotel in San Angelo. It seems the woman was incensed about some remark Raven made about her figure, and she attacked him.' Trace gave a shrug and sipped from his coffee cup. He continued, 'Raven was standing out on the balcony and Emma charged out, brandishing a knife. Raven ducked and Emma went over the balcony railing, landing on her head in the street below dressed only in her nightgown. Her neck was broken and they arrested him.'

'You'd think he could have found a way to stop her — a woman,' Sally said.

'You never saw Emma Goodwine,' Trace told her. 'She was a . . . hefty woman. She must have weighed two hundred and fifty pounds. She had the temper of a she-bear. Still the citizens of San Angelo gave some consideration to the fact that she was a female and decided that Raven, known rowdy that he was, deserved some prison time for her death.'

'Still . . . ' Sally said uncomfortably.

'Yeah,' Trace agreed with the unspoken remark. 'Still there was only Raven's word that things had happened the way he was telling it. Half the town thought that he should go free, the other half that he should be hanged for murder. You never do know with juries, but Raven wasn't very well liked in that town, running as he had with the Arista gang which had caused its share of trouble around San Angelo.

'The judge made a political decision and sentenced Raven to seven and a half years in state prison.'

Sally only nodded. She had not been there; who was she to sit in judgement? It did explain some of Raven's attitude toward women. Now Sally, too, glanced toward the river. She hesitated and then asked Trace, 'Woody Price — how does he fit into your plans? I mean, I can understand why you would want Raven along — he knows the gang's ways. If Woody was in prison as well, he, too, must be dangerous.' Her voice was uncertain. How could that young blond boy have found himself in the present situation?

'Woody is just a plain bank robber,' Trace replied. She thought he smiled, but it was only a faint twitch of his mouth. Darkness was settling, and Sally could not judge his meaning by his eyes. 'It was Raven who asked me to invite the kid along. He was Raven's cellmate in prison. He didn't think Woody belonged there, and asked me to help him.'

'But you said he was a bank robber,' Sally said in puzzlement. 'If that's so, why wouldn't he deserve a prison term?'

Trace told her, 'Woody rode to town with his two older brothers who told him that they had some business to take care of. Along the trail the two opened a bottle of whiskey and began hitting it pretty hard. Whether the liquor inspired them, or they had already made their decision, by the time they reached Midland, they were primed to rob the bank there.

'The two swung down in front of the bank and told Woody to hold their horses while they went into the bank to take care of their 'business'.

'Their timing couldn't have been worse. One of the town's deputy marshals was in the bank along with a local cattleman and two of his hands. All were armed. Shooting broke out and both of the Price boys were shot dead as they tried to run back to the bank door. Woody was found outside holding the ponies, and arrested on the spot.'

'But . . . ' Sally said hurriedly, for now she could see Raven and Woody returning from the river, leading the horses. 'If he didn't do anything . . . '

'The law doesn't make that distinction. He was there; he was involved. He got eight years in prison for his part in the robbery.'

'And so,' Sally said, 'Raven made a bargain with you for Woody's freedom. That was a kind gesture.'

'It was. I had no use for the kid, but Raven wanted him in on the bargain.' Trace rose to greet the two men back to the camp. He said in a low voice to Sally, 'Raven is erratic, but he's no heartless beast.'

'I appreciate you talking to me,' Sally said, meaning it. She rose and dusted off her skirt. She thought she understood these men a little better now. At least her fear of them had waned.

'Why are my ears burning?' Raven said as he entered the camp, walking directly to the coffee pot.

'You flatter yourself, Raven,' Trace Cavanaugh replied. Then, 'All right, I admit it. I was telling Sally what a fine all-around fellow you are . . . once someone gets to know you.'

Woody had sidled up to have a cup of coffee poured into his own tin cup by Raven. He seated himself not far from Sally, not near to her, spreading out his blanket. There was something different about him, Sally noticed. His hair was damp, combed back, and some of the raw smell of the trail was gone. She knew that men long on the trail were bound to smell of horses, sweat and man-scent, and she accepted it. Still, the fact that Woody had made the effort to clean himself up was appreciated.

'Somebody ought to get up above the tree line and keep watch for the Aristas,' she heard Raven saying, nodding toward the low cluster of willows surrounding them. 'We still don't know where they are, and I'd hate to have them bursting in here while I was sleeping.'

'Good idea, Raven,' Trace said evenly. 'I appreciate you volunteering for sentry duty.'

'What made you think I was volunteering?' Raven asked.

'Calm down,' Trace said, briefly resting a hand on the dark man's shoulder. 'We'll all take a turn.'

'Well, thanks,' Raven said with sarcasm. 'Do you mind if I finish my coffee first?'

Woody spoke from his cross-legged

position on the ground. 'I'll take the duty if you don't want it.' There was a sort of deference in his offer. No wonder, Sally thought, if not for Raven helping him, Woody would be spending this night locked up in prison. Their camaraderie seemed awkward but real. Living together day and night for years had forged a strong bond between the two.

'That's all right, kid,' Raven answered. 'You always did need your sleep more than me. I'll go.'

Trace Cavanaugh stood studying the stars. 'Come get me after midnight, Raven. I'll spell you.'

'Don't think I won't, boss,' Raven said, his white teeth flashing a grin in the starlight. He snatched up his Winchester rifle and walked off, making his way through the willow brush and cottonwood trees toward the river bank above them.

'You'd better break out whatever we have left in the way of provisions, Woody,' Trace said. 'I know I'm hungry;

our guest must be.'

It was poor food. A few salt biscuits, jerky and their coffee. Still Sally was grateful for it. She had not eaten since the night before. She had been thinking all day of the supper she had planned for her and Father — ham, sweet potatoes and greens. All of that had been destroyed in the fire of course. She pulled herself back from those dark thoughts and said, as she sat chewing on one of the hard biscuits, 'Well, they have three restaurants down in Sheffield. There might be more now. It's been awhile since I've visited there.'

Last Christmas, which it seemed was when Luke Cason made his annual withdrawal of funds from the stolen money. Had someone seen him in the bank and gotten to wondering? Sally's thoughts were darkening again. She asked brightly, 'Will we make Sheffield by tomorrow?'

'The day after at the earliest,' Trace said. 'Of course, we can't be certain that Regal Arista will be taking his men directly there. They could lead us off on a long false trail in the opposite direction.'

'But that's the only destination that makes sense, isn't it?' Sally asked, swallowing her biscuit, following it with tepid coffee.

'Yes, but I'm still not counting on it.'

'Like Raven and the deuces,' said Woody who had been inching closer to Sally. Trace nodded; Sally looked baffled.

'Tell her,' Trace said. Woody leaned back on his elbows. The evening was quiet, starlit. A million crickets were chirping along the river-bed. It was a moment before Woody began his story, gathering his thoughts. He knew he was not a natural storyteller and wanted to make sure he got it right. It was Raven's tale, but he had told it often enough to Woody back in their prison cell.

'This was back in San Angelo not long before Raven was arrested for killing the fat ... before he got arrested. He was sitting in a poker game with four other men — I can't recall all of their names, but one of them was a man he thought was a professional gambler named Karl Jewett.

'The game was five-card draw and Jewett's raises had bumped the other players out of the game as the stakes grew. Only Raven and Jewett were left holding cards at the table. Jewett hesitated to raise again — his stack of chips was down and he couldn't be sure what Raven was holding.'

Woody smiled. Sally waited, watching him — almost fondly, Trace thought. Woody went on with his story.

'There was this girl named Carrie Winkle working in the saloon at the time, a redhead without a lot of brains in her skull. She happened to be passing behind Raven carrying a tray with a load of empty beer mugs. She paused and shook her head, looking at Raven's hand, and said loud enough for anyone to hear, 'Nothing but deuces?'

'The look Raven gave her was cold enough to freeze her blood. She scurried away. Jewett, across the table, was smiling thinly. He shoved the remainder of his stack of chips into the middle of the table, calling Raven's bluff. Turns out Jewett was holding a full house, kings over fours, and he spread them on the table, reaching for the pile of bills, chips and coin there.'

Sally had to prompt him. 'And?' she asked.

'Carrie had been right. Raven was holding nothing but deuces — four of them. He fanned them out on the baize for Jewett to see. The man about had apoplexy. Raven stood drinks for half the town that night, bought Carrie a new dress, and himself a new suit and a new pony in the morning.'

'Yes,' Sally said, 'but is there a point to this story?'

Trace answered, his voice lazy with weariness. 'Yes, there is. It goes back to what you were saying about the Arista gang heading for Sheffield because they must be. No matter what you think you know, no matter what assurances you have, don't bet your last dollar on it. Men have been proven wrong believing they positively know the truth of matters.'

'But,' Sally said, 'the odds are — '

That was when the rifle fire crackling near at hand broke the silence of the night.

4

Trace flashed into motion instantly, although he did not rise to his feet. He grabbed his own rifle and kicked out the fire, smothering the clearing with darkness. Woody Price had rolled out of his blanket toward Sally and he now held her pinned to the ground, his Colt revolver in his hand, eyes anxious and alert.

There had been four shots fired, all from rifles, but how many men had been behind those shots? They remained still, shielded only by the night, waiting with silent apprehension.

Woody whispered, 'Where's Raven? Maybe I ought to go looking for him.' His concern was obvious.

Trace shushed him and hissed back, 'Raven knows what he's about.'

Did he? Sally wondered. She was pressed to the ground by the weight of

Woody Price's body. Oddly, she did not find it objectionable but comforting. This was a young man who obviously cared about his friends, and perhaps he now counted Sally among them. His protective substance was welcome in the night.

'Shh!' Trace Cavanaugh hissed again. They could see his eyes, fixed on a spot up the slope leading to the river-bank. The muzzle of the Winchester rifle in his hands had shifted that way.

Then Sally Cason, too, heard something moving in that direction. So did Woody, apparently, for his Colt revolver was now trained that way as well.

The sound became more reckless, disturbing, as if a group of men or an injured man were staggering toward their camp, forcing their way through the brush. Woody had thumbed back the hammer of his revolver. Sally curled herself into a tighter, primitively protective ball.

Raven emerged suddenly from the brush and called out, 'All clear, folks.

That extra horse we've been needing? Well, I've got him here.' And Sally saw the reason Raven's passing through the brush had been so noisy. He was leading a red roan with startled eyes.

'Whose is it?' was all Trace Cavanaugh asked, as he rose to his feet, dusting off his jeans.

'Ours, obviously.'

'Who did it used to belong to?' Trace asked, knowing Raven's sense for dramatic story telling. Raven led the red roan into the camp. The skittish animal was still shuddering.

'Bob Shelby used to ride a horse like this,' Raven said, with one of his broad white smiles. 'I don't think he'll be needing it any more.' He handed the reins to Sally who had struggled to her feet with Woody's assistance. 'Here,' Raven told her. 'You'd better let him get used to you. He's your horse now.'

Sally took the leather ribbons uncertainly and stroked the horse's muzzle, trying to calm it. The animal had been through a lot and she did not need a skittish steed.

'I should water it, too,' she said in the direction of Trace Cavanaugh. 'The other horses have had their drink.'

'I don't want you wandering off alone,' Trace said.

'I'll go down to the river with her,' Woody spoke up immediately, surprising no one.

'Get going, then,' Trace said. 'Me, I want to hear what Raven has to say.'

The two younger members of their party wandered off down the starlit path to the Pecos leading the roan. Raven grunted and said, 'Ain't love grand!'

'It can be,' Trace replied without any of Raven's sarcasm. 'You'd better tell me what happened, Raven.'

'What happened,' Raven replied, filling his cup with the nearly-cold coffee, 'is that I happened upon my old friend Bob Shelby up there.'

'Alone?'

'All alone, and he was obviously

riding wary — he had his Winchester across the saddlebow.'

'Then he was looking for us.'

'What else?' Raven asked.

'Seems odd, that's all. Maybe he was just trying to make his way to the river.'

Raven's dark eyes grew darker. 'What are you saying, Trace? All I know is that Bob spotted me and levered two shots at me. 'Course in this light he couldn't have known who I was. He just got spooked. I shot him out of the saddle. What would you have done?'

'The same,' Trace said. 'I'm just wondering what he was doing alone, away from the rest of the gang.'

'Who knows. Bob Shelby always was a little unpredictable. Maybe he quit the Aristas.'

'Just as they were about to reclaim that fifty thousand in gold — or whatever is left of it — from Luke Cason?'

'You're asking me questions I can't answer, Boss,' Raven said. He squatted on his heels, smiling up at Trace.

'You don't have to call me 'boss', you're not in prison now, you know.'

'I know it,' Raven said. 'It's just a habit. Those warders, they liked to be called that. After a few years it gets to be a habit of speech. Just like a man who's been in the army will keep on calling men 'sir' the rest of his life.'

'All right. I guess I might as well take my turn at watch now,' Trace said.

'You don't want to move the camp?' Raven asked.

'Because Bob Shelby might have found us?' Trace asked with tolerance. 'No — he didn't report his findings, did he? Besides, making a move would draw more attention to us than sitting still.'

'I suppose,' Raven said, tossing away the remains of his cold coffee. 'Say, boss, what's going to become of me and the kid if we don't manage to catch up with the Aristas and recover that gold?'

'That's not up to me, Raven.'

'But you'll have a say in it.'

'I'll be asked to make a recommendation for pardon or parole, but it's the governor and the parole board who'll have the final say.'

'But things will look better for us if we succeed.'

'Of course,' Trace answered. 'Now, better let me get off toward the bluff. There could be other riders up there.'

'Sure thing, boss. Keep your eyes open.'

'I always do,' Trace said flatly, and he started through the trees and willow brush toward the crest of the sandy bluff by starlight. The night was quiet and still comfortably cool. A few night birds were about, but those were the only sounds he heard as he reached the verge and found a place to settle in to watch the night plains. He was getting a little worried about Raven.

In the prison he had been all eagerness for a chance to prove himself, deferential and obliging in his manner. Now, it seemed that breathing the fresh air of freedom was bringing out another side of Raven — a little sarcastic, a little mean, a little obstinate. Had he really been forced to kill Bob Shelby, a man Raven had known well and ridden with for years? It seemed that Shelby had only happened to stumble upon their camp. Maybe Bob had severed ties with Regal Arista and the gang and had simply been looking for water. Or he could have been driven off by them to cut down the number of men splitting the pay-off from the fifty-thousand in that Sheffield bank. Maybe Shelby had not yet been a part of the gang when it held up the copper mine office over in Bisbee, Arizona, and made off with the payroll, and Regal had decided Bob should not have an equal share. Such things had been known to happen.

Only Raven might know. And that was the thing with Raven, his background and his pattern. For instance, only Raven knew what had really happened with Emma Goodwine down in San Angelo. You took his word or rejected it. Trace had been willing to take the convict's word because he needed his help to track down Aristas. Maybe Trace himself was being played for a fool. He did not wish to think that, but the possibility existed.

During the shoot-out between Raven and Bob Shelby, who had fired the first shots? According to Raven it had been Shelby and Raven had been forced to fire back to defend himself. Could Raven have recognized Shelby and simply ambushed him for reasons known only to the convict?

It depended on whose word you took. Bob Shelby was no longer present to offer his version of events.

Shifting a little to ease his position, Trace settled in for what was going to be a long night. What hand was Raven playing? Did he have more cards than he was showing?

There was nothing to be done about it. Trace himself had dealt the hand, but he felt now that he might be playing against a gambler known to be a consummate bluffer. Yes, Raven's advice to Trace to keep his eyes open might have been only obvious advice, or it could have been the convict's veiled warning of trouble sure to come. Trace grumbled, ground his teeth and sat waiting, watching the long, empty land for the trouble that was surely looming before him.

Sally Cason was the first one up in the morning. She stretched and walked out toward the river for privacy while she prepared for the day. The dawn was an odd coincidence of light and dark. Shadows were pooled heavily under the trees. The tips of the cottonwoods were burnished by the early morning light. The insects were already up — gnats, mosquitoes and iridescent dragonflies skimming low across the river. Silver fish breached the surface of the slate-gray Pecos. At the river's edge she saw a cottontail doe with a brood of a dozen young rabbits. Her approach sent them bolting into the underbrush.

There still had been no riverboat on the river; no hope of getting to Sheffield in that way. Would she be better off on a flatboat with unknown men? Sally did not know, but the men she now rode with were determined to track down her father and his kidnappers, and that was all she wanted to do.

The land beyond the river was much the same as it was on this side — long, empty, forlorn and beautiful at once. It wouldn't suit many young women, but it was Sally's home country and she loved it in a way she had never tried to define. It was home, that was all. It didn't seem to matter where you were from, how poor the country might be — home was simply better than other places.

Washing up as well as she could in the cold river water, she strode back to the camp where the men were up and stirring.

Woody had already saddled the red roan — Sally's red roan — for her. She could see that the saddle had been hastily wiped down. She did not wish to think about that. The roan seemed to be in a better temper this morning, calmed down from its experience of the night before, and it let her slip him the bit and stroke his muzzle without resistance.

Whoever Bob Shelby had been, he was a man who knew horses and took care of them. The roan was tall, strongly muscled, sleek and apparently intelligent. He looked to be a runner. Someone — probably her father — had told Sally that outlaws, successful outlaws, always owned the best horses to be found. They spent a lot of time trying to run from men whose horses were not quite so fine.

Keeping the horse's reins in hand, Sally walked nearer to the camp and thanked Woody for his efforts. He mumbled something shyly and turned away. Were women that frightening to him? Of course he had reached adulthood in a prison, without women. Raven was another matter. He did not glance at Sally but left his eyes riveted to her. There was an unhealthy glint in his eyes. Sally walked her horse to where Trace Cavanaugh was outfitting his big gray horse, his ice-blue eyes intent on his chore. As Sally approached, Trace was positioning his second scabbard.

She had noticed before that Trace's rig had his Winchester riding on the right side of his saddle and that a double-twelve shotgun was strapped to the left. She supposed it was not unusual for a man used to violent encounters, but she had never seen such a set-up.

Trace glanced up at her and nodded. He did not smile — he seemed a little unused to that expression. Perhaps he had seen too much in his career as a lawman. Nevertheless, Sally liked Trace Cavanaugh. He was strong, self-assured and competent, although it was covered with a rough exterior. He was probably gentle with women and children.

Did he have children? Was he married? She realized that Trace had not told her a word about his own life, only bits of Raven and Woody's. She supposed that men like him just did not share much of their personal thoughts and feelings.

Trace reminded her much of her father. That thought brought her worries to the surface again, and she asked Trace, 'Which way are we riding today?'

'Well, we gave some thought to trying to backtrack Bob Shelby, but wherever Arista was, he's probably gone by now.' Trace tilted his hat back. He was looking neither at her nor into the distances. 'I still think that they've got to be needing water, probably badly. They'll want to reach the Pecos at some point, or drive straight through to Sheffield, which as you were saying, the odds favor.

'If I were Regal Arista I'd want to have that money in hand as soon as possible. So, Sally, we're riding south. We'll keep close to the river, but not right along its banks — the brush screens vision too much.'

71

'Marshal Cavanaugh . . . ?' Sally said, trying to screw up her courage. 'If we cross their trail, will my father be in great danger?'

'Sally, Luke Cason is the last man they'd want to see killed.'

'I suppose,' she considered. If they wanted that gold, her father was their only chance to recover it. She wished someone would tell her how Luke Cason had come by that money in the first place, for now she was sure that everything Trace believed was the truth. The only man who would know was Raven, and Sally did not wish to strike up a conversation with the dark man.

The sky was still flushed with dawn light when they rode up from the river to the flat land beyond. Trace led the way with Raven near beside him. Sally followed on the red roan, keeping close to Woody on his buckskin.

They spotted a small herd of pronghorn antelope far to the south — probably they had been coming to the river to drink and been frightened at their approach. The graceful animals would circle around and come back. Sally was glad she was not among hunters, though there had been a time or two when she had been equally glad to see her father ride in with one of the slender animals across his saddlebow assuring them of meat to eat.

Sally watched the backs of the two men riding ahead. Trace seemed to ignore Raven when he tried to start a conversation. She wished that Woody, riding close beside her, would offer a few words, comments, but she was not surprised when he maintained his almost brooding silence.

Once, as the sun climbed higher into the sky and the long, featureless land began to heat once more, Woody did mutter as if to himself, 'If we don't find your father, I'm cooked.'

'What do you mean?' she asked, and Woody answered almost angrily.

'What do you think I mean? If we don't find him, we'll never recover the gold or capture the Aristas. I'm certain to be sent back to prison for another five years. I'd still be there if it weren't for Raven.'

'You're forgetting about Trace,' Sally said. Woody turned his heated glare on her.

'No, I'm not. I know that Trace is the man who had the key to the prison cell, but Raven is the one who talked him into using it.'

Sally asked, 'If Raven managed to find the money and somehow keep it for himself — what would you do, Woody?'

'What would I do?' Woody expelled a dry laugh. 'I don't know. That would give me the choice of going back to prison for five years or running off and living the high life somewhere with Raven. What would you do?'

'I don't know,' Sally said honestly. 'But if you ran away, you'd still be a prisoner of sorts — hunted down, maybe killed. If you stayed with Trace and did your best, he'd get you released.'

'Boss Cavanaugh doesn't have that kind of power — you heard him.'

Sally was startled to hear Woody Price using the pejorative 'boss' as Raven had, but she supposed that in prison every man's habits of speech became a part of each man's vocabulary. Woody had, after all spent two years locked in the same cell with Raven day and night. And what must that have been like for a simple farm boy!

'I think I'd rather live as a free man than be on the run for the rest of my life,' Sally said, turning her calm gaze on Woody.

'Easy to say if you're not in that situation. Besides, what makes you think Raven would break the bargain he's made with Trace?'

Sally didn't have an answer for that question. But she knew. She knew that if Raven saw his chance he would forget all about parole, the possibility of a pardon. He already had his freedom thanks to Trace taking a chance on him, and if his saddle-bags were filled with money, he would certainly make a break for it. That seemed to be always on Trace Cavanaugh's mind as well.

A second thought occurred to Sally, although Trace must have already known it and taken the risk with Raven. Was Raven planning on rejoining the Aristas? Then he could count on a cut of the money and would have some protection from pursuing lawmen.

What about Woody? Sally studied the young man's grim face. Would he go so far as to follow Raven to the Arista gang? Perhaps. She hoped not, but it was possible that Raven had planned this all and decided to offer Woody Price a proposition. For what reason? To have an extra gun along?

Sally found herself beginning to grow uneasy all over again. She let the red roan drift away from Woody's horse. She would wait until she had the chance to talk to Marshal Cavanaugh again before deciding, but she was beginning to believe that she would be better off away from these men. She now had her own horse and the river to follow to Sheffield.

Having their protection gave her a measure of security out in this broad, wild land. But what price security? In the worst possible imaginable scenario, she could conceive of Raven and Woody shooting the marshal in his sleep and running off with Sally in tow to meet the Arista gang. Then both she and her father would be bound to do whatever the outlaws dictated.

It was a stretch of the imagination, she knew, but it remained a possibility. Woody's guile could be feigned; Raven's smiling bonhomie had already shown its surface cracks. Sally swore to herself not to forget: she was riding a desolate land in the company of two convicts whose intentions were unknown, could not be guessed at. She knew one thing with certainty: Bob Shelby was not the last man who was going to be killed along this bloody trail.

5

'The horses are dragging their feet a little, Boss,' Raven said. He was smiling, but there was little humor in it.

The sun was riding high in a pale sky, heating a white land. Trace Cavanaugh nodded. 'They are,' he agreed. 'Let's let them rest awhile and have some water. I could use a little cool shade myself.' He slowed his gray horse long enough for the others to catch up.

'We're going to sit out midday along the river,' Trace told Woody and Sally, who was grateful for a respite from the heat and dust. A hot wind had risen late in the morning and continued to blow as they sat their sweating horses, discussing matters. 'Someone find a break in the brush so we can reach the river,' Trace told them.

It took a little time, but eventually Woody reported that he had found a place where the bluff had collapsed and formed a sort of sandy tongue stretching almost to the edge of the Pecos. They made their way along it and swung down in the welcome shade of the cottonwood grove that flourished on the river-bank. Saddle cinches were loosened and the horses led to water. Sally noticed that the marshal stood away from the others, watching just like a jailer — which he was. She walked to where he stood in the dappled shade.

'Sally, do you know of another settlement this side of Sheffield?' Trace asked.

'No, sir, I don't. My father and I never came this way. We only ever rode to Sheffield in December, as I told you, and there's always plenty of water to be found in the winter even in the rough country. Why do you ask?'

'Well,' Trace told her, 'I'm starting to get hungry, and I figure to be a lot hungrier before we reach Sheffield.'

'I know,' Sally said. Her own stomach was in agreement. Again she reflected on how much she missed her home, having a home. Looking toward the river where the horses stood in a row, their heads down, drinking, with Raven and Woody in what seemed to be close conversation, she asked, 'How much do you trust Raven? You told me that you did trust him.'

'Did I? I trust him to do what's good for Raven,' Trace replied. 'Riding with me and finding the Aristas was good for Raven. I'm almost certain both of them will be granted a pardon if we can find Regal Arista and recover the missing gold.'

'They don't seem so sure of that,' Sally commented. Trace's mouth tightened a little.

'I know, and the further we get from the prison the more they'll be thinking about riding off on me.'

'How many men ride for the Aristas?' Sally asked.

'Last I knew there were only six or seven of them left. They got into a shoot-out over in Odessa last year.

Almost the whole town turned out to join in the fight. Arista lost as many as a dozen men there.'

'The only one I've heard named is Regal Arista. Are the others known men?'

'Inside law enforcement circles they are,' Trace told her. 'Arturo, or 'Arthur' Arista is Regal's brother. They both rode up from Sonora years ago with a man named Rialto — he was one of those killed in Odessa. Bob Shelby was with them — you know what happened to him.'

She did, but, like Trace himself, she was not sure why.

'There's a man named Victor Segundo — a nice fellow who chopped up his wife with a machete in a drunken rage.' Trace saw Sally shudder. 'Then Monte Dixon is with them. Nice-looking man with a perpetual smile. He'll shoot you while he's smiling. He's not that good with a pistol, but he's diligent in applying one. Garret Black is plain mean. He's a thug with a face that

81

proclaims him for what he is: a nasty brute. Frank Corbett, who is slick with cards and with a knife. And probably still the Indian with no known name who acts as Regal Arista's personal watchdog, day and night he watches over him. It's said that Regal saved the man's life once — I wouldn't know, no one does. Of course some of these could be dead or retired now, in prison, gotten religion; a lot of others could have joined — but I doubt Arista wants new recruits along when they are ready to split up that fifty thousand. So there's probably only these six or seven men who've been with Regal from the start.'

'Sounds like a tough bunch,' Sally commented. 'I find it hard to believe that my father was ever among them.'

'It's hard to say how men get caught up in these things,' Trace said. 'You'd have to ask him about it.'

'But . . . is it only Raven's word that my father was riding with the Aristas?'

'Yes. But the evidence points that

way, doesn't it?'

'I suppose.' Sally was thoughtful for a few minutes, watching the wind ruffle the leaves of the cottonwood trees, looking toward the men who had now finished watering the horses and were leading them back.

'How can you hope to fight such a bunch, by yourself?'

'I'm pretty good at recruiting local lawmen to help out,' Trace answered. His eyes, too, were watching the two men with their horses. 'Not a lot of local constables, town marshals or county sheriffs are eager to shoot it out with a gang like Aristas, as much as they want them out of their territories.

'I just offer them a chance to be deputized as state marshals . . . or give them the choice of being charged with dereliction and obstructing a marshal in the performance of his duties.'

'You would do that?' Sally asked in amazement. Trace flashed one of his infrequent small smiles.

'I've never had to yet. But my

approach has had some success in the past. I usually end up getting cooperation from the locals.'

'You always get your man, is that it?' Sally asked lightly. 'One way or the other.'

'I always give it my best shot,' Trace replied.

'I'm going to drink my fill of water and sit in the shade,' Raven announced. 'I haven't seen this much sun for a long time.'

'Good idea,' Trace said. 'Maybe you boys could just rig up a string for the ponies between a couple of these trees first. We'll wait a few hours before we move on.'

Raven nodded and led the two horses he had away. Woody paused long enough to unfasten a lariat to use to secure the horses, then followed, his eyes glancing only once at Sally.

'Have you been quarreling with the kid?' Trace asked Sally.

'What have we got to quarrel about?' Sally answered in a way that let Trace know she considered it none of his business. Then she started out walking alone along the shaded river-bank.

The horses seemed contented enough, now tethered to the string, but Trace knew they must be wishing for graze. Well, they would have to suffer along with the humans for a little time longer.

Woody was back, seating himself on the ground near the base of a large cottonwood. He took off his hat and briefly fanned himself with it.

'Where's Raven?' Trace asked.

'Why, he's . . . ' Woody's voice faltered. 'I don't know. He wouldn't have taken off, not without his horse. I don't know where he is, boss.'

'I think we'd better find him,' Trace said with some alarm. 'Sally's gone out walking by herself.'

'Raven wouldn't . . . ' Woody began automatically, but then he rose swiftly to his feet and started down along the river bank with as much speed as he could muster. Trace snatched up his rifle and began circling through the brush and trees. He didn't know what Raven was up to, but he seemed to be growing more reckless with each passing mile.

It was vaguely possible that Raven intended to meet the Arista gang here. But that seemed a distant likelihood. Trace had to believe that Woody's instincts were right. Raven meant to surprise Sally in her walk. Why he would risk such a thing was unfathomable, but Raven was becoming erratic once more. He knew that Trace could not now turn around and return him to prison, not when they were this close to their goal. Unless he were planning on —

Trace heard the woman scream and he began running that way, crashing through the brush.

★　★　★

Sally had dipped her white scarf into the river, wrung it out and applied it to forehead, cheeks and neck. What she needed was a complete bath, but she didn't dare. The day was hot even in the shade, and the dry wind continued to torment the tree tops. Leaves rattled and spun off as tortured boughs creaked and moaned. The river, blue and silver in the sunlight flowed past swiftly as if making its way eagerly southward. Sally stood for a moment looking upriver, but there was no vessel afloat on the Pecos.

There was the snapping of a twig in the line of brush behind her, and she turned that way, expecting to see a deer or other animal making its way to the water. She was not expecting the animal with flushed face, eyes wild who burst upon her.

She managed to scream once before Raven's heated body collided with hers and she was jolted back against the sandy river bank. Raven's callused right hand was thrown over her mouth, his other was groping at her skirt. It was hard to breathe with his hand clamped over her face, impossible to squirm away with his full weight on her. She tried beating on his back, but her small fists seemed to have no effect.

His breath was hot, stale, his eyes savage. She was unwilling to surrender but unable to fight back. She closed her eyes for a moment, and when she opened them again, it was in time to see a second shape throw itself across the bank to collide with Raven, and both men went rolling away from her toward the water's edge.

Raven got to his feet, wearing a nasty grin. He stood there panting as Woody Price flung himself at Raven again, both arms flailing. A right-hand fist caught Raven flush on the mouth, splitting his lower lip, a following left struck his nose, starting blood leaking from his nostrils. Raven backed away, circling. Sally could see that Woody's gun had been shaken loose of its holster. It lay dully gleaming on the sand.

'Listen, kid,' Raven said, placing both of his hands up at shoulder level. 'You don't know what you're doing.'

Woody grunted something that was barely human and threw himself at Raven again, his thin blond hair flying. Raven stopped the rush with a straight left jab which snapped Woody's head back, but did nothing to convince him to quit.

Woody's hooking fists caught Raven twice again on either side of his jaw, and the convict staggered back.

'That's about enough out of you,' Sally heard Raven growl, and she saw that he had drawn his Colt revolver.

'That won't stop me!' Woody shouted.

'Oh yes it will,' Raven answered. 'It's stopped a hell of a lot better men than you.'

Woody stood slightly hunched forward, hair in his eyes, panting. His fists were still clenched into tight balls. Despite Woody's passion, he knew that there was no point in rushing Raven's cocked revolver. He glanced once at Sally and said to Raven in a voice that squeaked a little with stress, 'I should have just killed you when I had the chance.'

'That's a lesson for you to learn,' Raven said coldly, wiping at his blood-smeared face.

'I've a lesson for you,' Trace's voice put in. 'Do you want to learn it, Raven, or are you going to drop your gun?'

The marshal was standing twenty feet away, his rifle to his shoulder, the Winchester's sights fixed on Raven.

There was only the briefest hesitation before Raven's fingers opened and his pistol dropped to the ground. He knew that Trace Cavanaugh would pull that trigger. 'Oh, the hell with it,' Raven said, managing to smile. 'The kid got everything wrong and just went crazy. I came along and saw the girl stumbling as she tried to get up the bank from the river. I caught her and we both fell.'

'That's a lie,' Sally said. Her voice quavered, and she had to sit down on the ground; her legs were still trembling.

'A hysterical woman,' Raven said with a shrug. 'You know women, Trace, they'll say anything to get you on their side.'

'Will they?' Trace's voice was colder than Sally had heard it before. He slowly lowered the rifle. 'Woody,' he said, 'gather up those handguns. We'd better get back to camp. Someone might have it in mind to grab our ponies.'

'I'm not giving him back his gun,' Woody said defiantly.

'I didn't tell you to. Come on — let's get going. Raven, you can do me the favor of leading the way.'

'You've got me all wrong, boss,' Raven said, as he passed by to take the lead along the trail. Trace didn't bother to answer.

'It's the kid — he made a mistake,' Raven tried as they walked through the mottled shade toward their camp. 'He just went kind of crazy. After all I've done for him.' Raven sounded genuinely disappointed in Woody Price. He shook his bloody head miserably.

Trace didn't bother trying to sort Raven out. He only said, 'These things can happen when a woman is involved.' He left it to Raven to make what ever he liked of the comment.

'I was his best friend,' Raven said miserably. Then he repeated it as the four trudged in a line back to camp, 'His best friend.'

Despite the disturbance, Trace decided to wait a few more hours before starting out again. The sun was still high and hot; the horses could use a little more rest. Let emotions cool some. Raven seated himself, his back to a tree and sat glowering — chiefly at Woody Price. He would not forgive the kid easily, it seemed. Twice more he tried to convince Trace himself that it had all been a mistake on Woody's part, that he was not trying to harm the girl. Eventually he gave up the fiction.

Raven had watched with his dark hooded eyes as Trace placed the convict's revolver in his saddlebags. 'You're going to need me and my gun if we run into the Aristas,' Raven muttered. His words were muffled and indistinct. His split lip had swollen and it seemed that speaking was painful to him.

'If we see them, I'll give it some consideration,' Trace answered. He too had seated himself against a cotton-wood tree. His hat was pulled down over his eyes. 'Count yourself lucky I haven't tied you up, Raven, and let you ride like that all the way to Sheffield.'

Sally had settled on the ground not far from Trace. She picked up a small twig and began breaking it into smaller pieces. As Raven closed his eyes and seemed to sleep and Woody paced nearer the river, she asked Trace a question.

'Can't you just arrest him now?'

'He's already under arrest, Sally. Remember? What would I do with him if I preferred a new charge? Leave him in the jail in Sheffield? I might need

Raven to identify some of the gang members. There could be some I haven't heard of that he knows on sight. Then I would be responsible for taking him back to the prison in shackles, which would be the same as admitting that I had made a terrible mistake in obtaining his release in the first place. They would never allow me to pull such a play again — even when I knew a man could point me to a murderer.

'No, Sally, this is an experiment that is going wrong, but I'm still responsible for it. You could always prefer charges against him — but I think it would be difficult to disprove Raven's own story since no actual . . . damage to your person occurred. I've seen Raven charm people including juries before.'

'Including you,' Sally said, trying to get a glimpse of Trace's eyes behind his tugged-down Stetson.

'I believed Raven because I wanted to,' Trace said. 'Shows you how dumb a man can be. But I want the Arista gang swept off the plains. I want to recover the stolen gold. And now . . . I want to find and rescue Luke Cason. I wouldn't have gotten this close if Raven hadn't guessed the gang was heading this way.'

Sally nodded her head, and finding another twig suitable for breaking, she got to her tiny task. 'If I did chose to prefer fresh charges, surely Woody would . . . '

What would Woody surely do? Stand by Raven out of friendship or some prison code? What weight would one convict's word carry against that of another convict in court? Sally resigned herself to the situation as it stood. Let Trace Cavanaugh handle matters as he wished.

As Woody returned from the river he looked at Trace and then at Sally. His eyes then flickered to the miserable sight of the dozing, battered Raven across the clearing. Sally rose and walked a little away from the camp.

Trace seemed to sense Woody hovering over him. Without raising his hat, he asked, 'What's on your mind, Price?'

Woody stood rubbing his knuckles. He had tried soaking his hands in the cold river, but they still ached.

Woody crouched, tilted back his hat and said quietly, 'Just this, boss, I feel real bad about hitting Raven. Maybe the whole thing was a mistake and Raven was telling the truth.'

Trace sat up just a little straighter and adjusted his hat so that he could look into the earnest eyes of the young Woody Price.

'Let me tell you a little of what I know about liars, Woody. They tell their lies as a matter of habit, and if the lie doesn't work, they start working on the honest types of this world, trying to make them feel guilty about disbelieving the lie. They often give the liar the benefit of the doubt, as they call it, and start worrying that they might have been wrong in accusing a man themselves.

'Raven is a habitual liar, and usually an adept one. That's why he immediately turned to the ploy of claiming himself as your only friend, a friend who had turned on him. He wanted to get you to where you were feeling, as you are now, that you might have been wrong somehow. You're not: you know what you saw.'

'I understand, boss,' Woody said in a low uncertain voice, 'but Raven really was just that: my only friend.'

'Well, friends don't lay that sort of guilt on a man, Woody. He was never your friend — just someone you've known for a long time. You've reached the point where you have to decide if you want men like Raven as friends out of loyalty, or want to move on and make new and better friends.'

Sally's return caught both men's attention and ended the conversation. Woody strode away to sit by himself in the shifting shade of the cottonwood trees.

The sun had begin to lower its head; the shadows beneath the trees were growing long, pooling together when Trace decided it was time to move on.

They were gaining no ground on Regal Arista and his bunch this way.

Saddled and outfitted once again they mounted the bluff to the flat land where the heated wind still blew. Trace spotted a pair of dust devils in the distance, spinning their way across the land.

Trace said, 'Raven, I'll show you the courtesy of letting you lead off.'

Raven smiled. 'Mind showing me the courtesy of handing me back my Colt?'

'Lead off,' Trace answered, and Raven started his black horse southward once more.

Woody rode beside Raven as they started on. Old bonds, Trace reflected, were hard to break.

'He seems to be apologizing to him,' Sally said in disbelief.

'Raven's had time to refine his story by now. Woody wants to believe that he, and not Raven, is the wrong-doer.'

'But why . . . ?' Sally was incensed and then she let her temper cool. She obviously did not understand men and especially convicts. She guided the red roan on, sitting the saddle easily despite the encumbrance of her skirts.

She asked Trace, 'Is there any chance we'll make Sheffield tonight?'

'I don't think so, not if I've got the geography of the land right. How long did it take you and your father to ride there from the ranch?'

'I don't know, really,' Sally answered. 'It was always like a long picnic to me. Spending a lot of time with Father, knowing that the annual ride meant that Christmas was near and I would return from town with presents and maybe a new dress . . . ' Speaking of it was suddenly not bearable.

'There will be other Christmases,' Trace said. 'With your father. I promise you.'

There was nothing like making hollow promises, Trace thought, but his words seemed to comfort Sally a little.

The day continued hot, monotonous as they trailed south. There was little in the way of plant life or animals. As the sky began to redden in the west the devil wind, thankfully, died down. The first star blinked on, gleaming wearily in the purple haze of dusk.

'Another night . . . ' Sally began to complain, but now ahead they saw Woody stand up in his stirrups and point vigorously toward the river. Sally was going to say that she couldn't take another night in the wilds without food, with these men around her, but she fell silent, stunned by the sight of a tiny village abutting the river's edge lying just ahead of them.

'I thought there wasn't a town before Sheffield,' Trace said.

'I never knew of one, but I told you Father never brought me this way. I don't think it can have been here long.'

'Maybe not,' Trace agreed. Towns in the West were founded, built up hopefully, abandoned and fell into disrepair before anyone knew they had ever been there.

'What are we going to do?' Sally asked.

'There's got to be someone down there who has food and hay for the animals,' Trace told her. 'We're going to see what we can find.'

The town, as they learned from a newly painted, rough sign, was called Donovan's Landing. There didn't seem to be more than a dozen structures altogether: tumbledown, slapped together affairs every one, but Donovan's Landing was nevertheless a welcome sight, a smidgen of civilization to the trail-deprived bunch.

They walked their ponies down the main street such as it was. Halfway along, Woody cried out enthusiastically. 'I smell somebody burning steaks!'

Woody was right, and they swung down and entered a low-ceilinged, long room where rows of men sat at trestle tables, hunched over platters of beef steak, beans and boiled potatoes. Men looked up with curious, speculative eyes as Sally entered the place, but their attention soon returned to the action of their forks and knives.

'What do you think, Sally?' Trace asked.

'I think if we can find a place to sit, it's time to eat.' She paused. 'But can we afford it?'

'I've got a steady job, remember. And I drew some traveling expenses for the boys and myself. Find an open spot on the bench, and we'll try to do justice to the food.'

After a heavy meal they went out on to the starlit night. They had asked about and been informed of where to find a stable and a boarding house. The horses came first and they were led into an unusually fresh-smelling horse barn by a narrow, arthritic man who moved with a cane.

The stable had seen little use, it seemed. There were only three or four other horses there. The strewn straw was clean. The horses followed the stableman eagerly to the stalls.

The boarding house — hotel, as the sign on the door proclaimed it — was a welcome sight, as the travelers were a welcome sight to the proprietor. 'Have you got rooms for us?' Trace asked at the desk. 'We'll require accommodations for four.'

The clerk, who had spiky, unbrushed reddish hair and looked as if he had just been awakened, grew eager. His eyes brightened as he replied, 'Yes, sir. Certainly, sir.'

Trace thought it must have been a while since four customers had come in at once. One room for Trace, one for Sally, and one each for Raven and Woody — Trace did not know what sort of mood existed between the two now; it was best that they sleep separately — came to eight dollars which Trace gladly paid. It would be well worth it for a good night's sleep under shelter.

With his stomach full and his room relatively comfortable, relatively safe, Trace Cavanaugh was barely into his bed covered by a single woven blanket when he drifted off into a deep sleep.

He was dreaming that he was in

some strange little valley where birds of all sorts clustered in the forest. Abruptly they flew off as if he had done something to startle them. All but a single redheaded woodpecker which remained behind and repetitively, annoyingly worked at the bark of a pine tree. Trace wanted to shoo the bird away, to shout at it to shut up, but these efforts are seldom possible for a dreaming man.

He watched the stupid bird in irritation until he could take no more. He shook his body awake, opened his eyes to a stream of bright morning sunshine leaking into the room through nearly-closed curtains.

The tapping continued.

Grabbing his pistol from its bedside holster, Trace made his way to the door of the room where someone continued to knock frantically. Holding his pistol beside his leg, he swung the door open a few inches to see Sally, her face distraught, her hair sleep-tousled, standing there, a blanket clutched around her. Her eyes were wide, her mouth grim.

'What . . . ?' Trace began to ask.

'They're gone!' Sally told him. 'Both of them. Raven and Woody, they've slipped off in the night.'

6

'Just a moment,' Trace said, and he turned to find his jeans and tug them on before he opened the door wide to allow Sally Cason to enter. 'Sit down and explain this. You say my two convicts are gone? How do you know?'

Sally sat in the single wooden chair in the room, gulped a few times and told her story as Trace parted the curtains and glanced out at the Pecos River, glittering in the morning light.

'I thought this morning that I would talk to Woody to see how things stood between us . . . ' She blushed. Trace nodded. No one had said that there was anything between the two young folks, but all of the evidence was there. He was hardly surprised. Sally continued in a rush of words.

'When I went to his room and knocked on the door shortly after dawn, my tapping swung the door open. I looked in to find him gone. Well, I thought, he's risen early and gone over to get some breakfast — but I knew he had no money.

'Raven's room was right across the hall, as you'll remember. I glanced that way to see that his door was slightly ajar, too. I sort of crept across the corridor and opened the door. Raven was gone as well.

'Where could they be?' Sally asked.

'We'll find out,' Trace promised her. He thought he already knew. His two prisoners had broken their promises and were now embarked on a race to find the money that was being held in the Sheffield bank. Did they hope to join up with Regal Arista? Possibly. Maybe they had come up with a new, clever idea of how to get the loot. Trace couldn't discount that — Raven was a cunning man.

Trace said, 'Get dressed and let me do the same. We'd better get moving as soon as we can.'

Having no luggage except for Trace's saddlebags, it took them no time at all to leave their room and meet down in the hotel lobby. Sally had taken the time to brush her hair and tie it back loosely with a piece of string.

'Maybe they were just both feeling restless and wanted to walk out this morning,' Sally suggested hopefully. The desk clerk suppressed that dim hope.

'They went out about midnight,' he told Trace. 'I assumed they were going to the saloon. So many of our guests do that after they've assured themselves of having a place to sleep.' The man had no further curiosity or interest in the movements of Raven and Woody Price — he had been paid in advance.

'What now?' Sally asked.

'We can hope they left our horses.' Trace answered. Sally hurried along on her small boots as Trace strode toward the stable. Even if their horses were still in the stable, Raven and Woody now had about an eight-hour lead on them. They would never catch them before they reached Sheffield. Sheffield town didn't know what was coming its way — a congregation of convicts and killers, and now Trace would not even be in time to warn the local law. Of course this also meant that Trace Cavanaugh would never be trusted again to try such a dangerous gambit. But that was secondary to ending the reign of terror the Aristas had exerted over this section of west Texas for years.

And to rescuing Sally's father from them.

They found Trace's gray horse and the red roan Sally had been riding in the stable. Probably Raven had weighed the benefits of and trouble of taking them along, and decided that it wasn't worth it. Besides, Raven knew that Trace had the money to buy two new horses if he were of a mind to.

'Well, that's something to be grateful for,' Sally said as they paid the stable hand and equipped their ponies.

'But we'll never catch up with those two,' Trace said. 'Not before Sheffield.'

'Maybe . . . ' Sally was hesitant, her small pink tongue was thrust out as she became thoughtful. 'What's the matter with my first idea, Marshal?' she asked Trace.

'Which idea was that?' Trace had to ask. Sunlight beamed brightly into the stable. Sally looked like a bright child who has come up with the solution to a perplexing problem.

'Well,' she said eagerly, 'what's the name of this town?'

'Donovan's Landing,' Trace said, still not making the connection.

'And what is that tied up to the pier at the end of the street — or didn't you notice? There's a flatboat waiting there. Probably it's going downriver to Sheffield.'

'We could find out,' Trace said thoughtfully. 'But let's do it quickly. We haven't any time to waste.'

They met the master of the boat standing on the pier. He was a round man with a red nose like a rubber ball and a set of white chin whiskers that bushed out wildly. Yes, he agreed, that was his boat.

'Name's Donovan,' he said around a wad of tobacco. Trace thought this might be some good luck. He asked the man:

'Are you going downriver soon?'

'Can't say.' Donovan scratched at his whiskers as if looking for small invaders concealed there. He spat and looked at the shambles of a town. 'I've a lot of interests around here. This is my town, Donovan's Landing. I built it.'

Trace had guessed that. It was only of passing interest. Getting downriver to Sheffield was a more immediate concern. 'Can you get us to Sheffield today?' he asked.

'That I can't say either,' Donovan replied, spitting off the pier into the water. The Pecos River flowed smoothly past. Its current appearing quick. Much quicker than the negotiations were going. It came to Trace that he had not been hitting the right note. He tried again.

'How much will you take to deliver us and our horses downriver to Sheffield.'

'Fifty dollars — in gold,' Donovan said without any hesitation.

Trace didn't know if that was exorbitant or not; he only knew they had to get to Sheffield, if not before Raven, then soon after. The coins he drew from his pocket glittered brilliantly in the morning sunlight.

'Those horses don't have heavy feet, do they?' Donovan asked. 'I can't have them frisking about and canting my keel.'

'They're placid beasts,' Trace told Donovan, who now had a worried look on his face. He accepted the gold coins, tucked them away and smiled again.

'Get the horses aboard then; we'll be leaving shortly. You can trice them up abaft the fo'c'sle.'

Sally looked bewildered. Trace was no less so. They saw a younger man with a black beard standing above them on the boat. He grinned and waved them aboard. They led the horses up the ramp provided, and looked around in confusion.

'I know he told us what to do with the horses,' Sally whispered, 'but I couldn't understand half of what he was saying.'

'Neither could I,' Trace admitted. The younger black-bearded man had approached them, still grinning.

'Don't pay any attention to Donovan's manner of speech. He was an open sea sailor for a long time until he grounded his ship off Galveston in a hurricane and they blamed him for its loss. What he said was that you can tie your horses up behind that shack. That's the fo'c'sle to Donovan. There's a row of iron rings bolted to the structure. Pigs, sheep, goats and horses have always been tethered there.

'My name's Bo Higgins,' the bearded man said. 'I've been touring the river with Donovan for almost a week.' Trace nodded to the helpful young man.

'I'm Sally Cason,' Sally said, 'glad to meet you — and thanks for the translation.'

Higgins grinned and shuffled away, hands in his pockets. 'What did you do that for?' Trace asked roughly.

'Do what for?' Sally asked, surprised. 'Introduce yourself?'

'I've always been taught that it's only proper to give your name to someone who introduces himself to you.'

'Not if your name happened to be Sally Cason,' Trace said. They had reached the rear of the crude shack that served as the flatboat's cabin, and Trace tied the horses to the black iron rings bolted to the wall.

'I can't see . . . I'm sorry, Trace but Bo Higgins is only a river rat. He can have nothing to do with our troubles.'

'Just keep our business to yourself until you and your father are safely away from this mess.'

His voice was so stern that Sally was taken aback. She realized only then how concerned Trace was about the Aristas and Raven. And her father. Trace would take it as a personal defeat if things went totally wrong — and it would be just that. This had all been his plan and the prison officials must have been dead set against it. Perhaps his own office had argued against its wisdom. But Trace had gotten his way, possibly to his own detriment.

Donovan, once properly motivated, wasted no time in casting off and within minutes they were in mid-stream on the Pecos, sailing rapidly southward. Sally said, 'We're bound to beat them there at this rate. There are no rocks and gullies on the river, no clumps of cactus and brush thickets to ride around.'

'We're making better time — we would never have caught up with them over land. Still, they have an eight-hour lead on us. Even on tired ponies, they have covered a lot of ground by now.'

'What about the Aristas, Marshal? Where are they?'

'That's a good question for which I

have no answer. It's barely possible that they have gone to the bank already and forced your father to access his deposit box. I don't think they've had enough time, but you never know. If they're careful doing what they have in mind, the law in Sheffield won't even be aware that they've been there.'

'And they won't even have committed any crime,' Sally said, pondering the swiftly flowing silver-blue river, the banks where the silver willows and cottonwood trees clustered. 'But won't they draw attention to themselves — that many armed men riding into town in a bunch? Some of them, Regal Arista in particular, are wanted men, you told me.'

'They won't ride in as a gang. Probably some of the men will camp outside town and others will filter in singly or in pairs in order to be there just in case there is any trouble.'

Sally nodded, mulling it over. She was glad she did not have all of Marshal Cavanaugh's concerns. All she wanted was for her father to be safe. A thought occurred sharply to her: 'After Father has done what they want, he'll be . . . expendable, won't he?'

'He'll be unnecessary,' Trace said, choosing a different word. 'He'll have to try to figure some way not to be forced to ride from town with the Aristas.'

'He could start yelling for the law,' Sally said with a hint of panic in her voice. Trace was no help.

'He'll have a gun on him at all times. I don't think Regal will want to leave him behind to tell his tale.'

'But why would he tell? If my father was involved in the copper mine robbery?'

'Maybe out of a hunger for revenge. His house has been destroyed. For all he knows you are dead. He might think that implicating every member of the gang in the crime and seeing them sent off to prison would be worth it. I really can't speak for what he might do; I don't know your father that well.'

After a silent minute as the flatboat

scudded along the face of the silver river, Sally said, 'I guess I don't know him that well either.'

For some time Trace had been aware of another figure standing close to them. Not near enough to hear what they were saying, or was he? The silence of the river was vast. Trace turned his head to see Bo Higgins watching them with a thoughtful expression. The younger man was near the horses. He inclined his head slightly indicating that he wished to speak with Trace.

Now what?

When Trace walked across the deck to where Bo Higgins waited, his arm thrown on to the back of Sally's red roan, the bearded man said in a low, conspiratorial voice, 'Marshal, I'd like to volunteer.'

Trace Cavanaugh slowly turned his eyes on the young Bo Higgins. He framed his answer carefully.

'I didn't need any volunteers for anything. Why did you call me 'Marshal'?'

'That's what Miss Cason called you — you see, Marshal, I do have a few faults — I am an eavesdropper. Anything anyone says is interesting to me out on the river. There's little else to occupy the mind.'

'I see,' Trace said. At the rear of the boat Donovan stood guiding the flat-boat with the tiller, his face set in a glum expression. No, there wouldn't be much conversation aboard this boat. 'What else did you happen to overhear, Bo?'

'The Aristas. I heard that you're going after them,' Bo Higgins said, his eyes over-bright with eagerness.

'Anything else?' Trace asked. He was still unsmiling. He didn't like his plans being spread about. He had tried to caution Sally, but she did go on — a little too much, it seemed.

'Just about everything you two said,' Higgins told Trace. 'Marshal, I'm not a boatman by nature. It just seemed to be the best way to work my way south. I'd give anything to have a pony under me again. And the Arista gang — they all have a price on their heads, don't they? I figure that would be a way for a man with nerve to make himself some money.'

'Law officers and their deputies can't collect rewards.'

'Well, no — though I hear a lot of them do rig it so they can collect,' Bo went on. 'But if I was just to go with you as a sort of friend of the law, without a badge or anything, I could still claim a reward, couldn't I?'

'I suppose. I really don't know for certain. It's never come up before.'

'Well, sure!' Bo Higgins said with confidence. 'Why if I could nail that Frank Corbett, for instance — I saw a wanted poster on him offering a five-hundred dollar reward — that would give me a good stake to start out on.'

'Higgins,' Trace said with patience. 'There's a poster out on Frank Corbett for good reason: he's a killer. They all are. Shoot at the Aristas and they'll shoot back. There are no guarantees in the line of work you're talking about. I can't tell you how many dead would-be bounty hunters I've known. It's a business for a desperate man who can't find any other decent work.'

'And what do I look like, Marshal?' Bo Higgins spread his arms. 'Do you think I want to spend my life like this? Forget all of the reward business. Pay me a dollar a day, or whatever you pay your deputies and let me ride with you. You surely aren't taking that gang down by yourself.'

Trace didn't answer. The kid was right in that respect. He seemed sincere enough in his desire to give up the river life. Trace had had stranger offers before, and some of them had turned out well. Still he did not know Bo Higgins, not well enough to trust him. But the kid was right about one thing: Trace was going to need some deputies, and he had no idea how well the law in Sheffield was going to co-operate, if at all. He again studied the black-bearded youth's eager face. He couldn't decide what to tell him. Apparently his judgement was not at its best these days. After all he had trusted Raven and Woody Price. In the end he managed to tell Bo, 'We'll talk about it in Sheffield if you're going to be staying over there.'

Bo Higgins was neither elated nor crushed by Trace's answer. There was a chance for him, his eyes seemed to be saying. He smiled, nodded his thanks and sauntered toward the rear of the flat boat where Donovan was calling for relief from his task.

Sally returned from wherever she had been. She had a glazed look in her eyes, possibly from staring across bright water, perhaps because she had had no hat to wear the past few days to keep the sun off.

'I saw you talking to Mr Higgins,' Sally said, 'I didn't want to interfere. What did he want?'

'To go along with me hunting the Aristas.'

'Well, that's what you need, isn't it? Deputies?'

'Deputies I know, or who come recommended by the local law officer.'

'How would you know you could trust them?' Sally asked. Trace paused a moment before he was forced to agree.

'You never can tell what a man will do when the shooting starts, or when there's a large sum of money involved.'

'Well, then,' Sally said with a small shrug, turning her eyes up to meet his gaze, 'Higgins seems as trustworthy as anyone else.'

'Just because he's attracted to you?' Trace teased. 'Look how Woody Price affected your judgement.' Sally seemed to blush. Her eyes turned down and away.

'I don't know what happened with Woody. He fought Raven for my honor, didn't he?'

'I suppose,' Trace commented meaninglessly. He was looking downriver intently. By his rough calculations of their speed, he believed they would

123

reach Sheffield within the hour. They began to see pecan trees crowding the shore now. In the early days pecan nuts were seen as nothing more than fodder for the hogs, like acorns, but the first frontier woman who'd baked a pecan pie changed that for good and all.

'We have to find you a place to stay, first thing,' Trace said.

'There must be some sort of hotel there,' Sally answered.

'Some more permanent sort of place.'

'For an impermanent girl,' Sally said. 'One who doesn't know if she will ever see her father again, or if you might be shot in some back alley.'

'Yes,' Trace said flatly, 'exactly that. You used to come down here with your father. Didn't he know anyone in town?'

'Only my aunt,' Sally said, her mouth drawing in tightly. The words came as a relief to Trace — Sally's welfare would be one less thing he had to worry about.

'You have an aunt who lives in Sheffield?'

'I think so,' Sally said doubtfully. 'I always accepted Sheila Warner as that when I was younger. She was kind enough to me, and extremely fond of my father. As I got older I began to wonder if Sheila was really my aunt or just some old . . . friend from my father's past.'

'Under the present circumstances, it doesn't really matter, does it?' Trace asked. Sally wagged her head slowly.

'We'll find this woman — if not tonight, tomorrow, and explain the situation.'

'And you'll have me off your hands?' Sally asked in a low voice.

'Exactly. You can be of no help to me, and I can't be of any further aid to you. I must get to work and try to complete my job.'

'Your killing job,' Sally said harshly.

'That's all up to the Aristas. They set the rule of the game themselves.' After another silent minute of watching the silver river flow past the heavy stands of trees, Trace asked, 'Sally, if your father were somehow able to shake free of Regal Arista, would he seek shelter at Sheila Warner's?'

'I can't think of another place in Sheffield where he would be welcome.'

That gave Trace cause to consider, and while he was still considering the boat swung around a bend in the river, the town of Sheffield suddenly appeared huddled along the banks of the Pecos River.

It had been a hell of a trip, but it was now at an end. Now the killing would begin.

7

With Sally checked into the Sheffield
Hotel, a white clapboard affair with
sun-peeled paint on the eastern wall,
and the horses stabled, Trace started
out toward the town marshal's office.
Bo Higgins dogged his tracks. Bo had
not been invited, but he had firmly
attached himself to Trace. Not only
that, he had given Donovan his notice
as they were leading their horses down
the ramp to the dock. Higgins had
spoken in unmistakable, perhaps unfor-
givable, terms about Donovan and life
on the riverboat. Bo had followed them
uptown and attached himself again to
Trace on his way to the town marshal's
office. You had to give the young man
credit for his persistence. Trace hadn't
bothered to try chasing him off. What
would have been the point of it?

The Sheffield town marshal was fat,

slovenly, nearly bald. His right leg was encased in plaster. His eyes were sharp, tiny, annoyed as Trace entered. Trace had pinned his badge on his shirt before entering and this seemed to be what was causing the marshal's annoyance.

'State police, huh?'

'That's right,' Trace said, seating himself in a wooden chair without having been invited. The office was small, airless, painted a drab green. There was a map of Texas on one wall, much faded and yellowing, and a few wanted posters pinned to a board. A rack of shotguns and Winchester rifles, all appearing slightly dusty, was near by.

'I don't recall asking for any help.' the marshal said, shifting his broken leg slightly.

'You didn't. I'm here to ask for your help. The name's Trace Cavanaugh, by the way. Marshal . . . ?'

'Dandridge.' The man answered as if it pained him. He sucked at his lower lip for a minute before asking warily,

'What sort of help are you talking about?'

'I have reliable information that the Arista gang is making its way toward Sheffield — if they're not already here.'

That seemed to shake Dandridge a little. No town marshal wants to think that his town is about to be invaded by a rough bunch of outlaws. 'You mean they might already be in Sheffield?' Dandridge asked with an attempt at a laugh. 'I think I would have noticed that.'

Maybe he wouldn't have; the marshal seemed pretty well rooted to his chair.

'I think they might come in singly or in pairs. Some of them might remain outside town at some camp, but Regal Arista certainly will show here.'

'What are they after? Our bank? The freight office? Is it a personal vendetta of some sort?' Dandridge asked, looking less smug and self-confident than he had before the name Arista had been brought into the conversation. 'Is that

Garret Black still with them? I had a meeting with that ugly thug once . . . '

'They don't intend to pull any sort of crime here,' Trace said, calming the marshal, bringing back his puzzlement.

'Then, they can come and go and be damned,' Marshal Dandridge said.

'They're all wanted men,' Trace reminded him.

'Capturing them isn't my responsibility; my job is protecting this town, that's all. The rest is up to the Rangers, or men like you.'

'Exactly,' Trace said, keeping his voice calm. He removed his hat and his graying hair escaped in a tangle. 'That's why I'm here, Dandridge. I'm out to bring down Regal Arista and his whole bunch — at least as many as I can take. But the odds are not good. Maybe six, seven to one.' That was without counting Raven and Woody Price, and Trace had to assume the two convicts had gone over to Arista.

'I'm a crippled man,' Dandridge said, rapping his knuckles against the plaster cast on his leg. 'I don't see what help I could be.'

Even if he wished to try, Trace was thinking, which apparently he did not. He could try his old bullying tactics on Dandridge, but somehow he did not think the town marshal would budge from his position. He was wearing his excuse on his leg.

'It doesn't have to be you personally,' Trace said. 'I just need a few able-bodied, willing men to back me. How about your deputies?'

'I've got two full-time deputies, Marshal Cavanaugh, and I need them both to patrol the town and keep order in Sheffield. That's what they're paid to do.'

'You must know other men who might be willing to help.'

'Not off-hand,' Dandridge said as if it pained him. 'Our citizens have their own business to attend to. I could send out a general call, but you know what kind of riff-raff you'd get: saddle bums, kids looking for excitement, drunks and old men with nothing else to do. They wouldn't be much help. Are you offering any wages, Cavanaugh?'

'I'm not authorized to do that,' Trace admitted unhappily. Dandridge's hands flew up and parted in a flying maneuver.

'Then what can I tell you — except to wish you good luck.'

Trace rose, planted his hat and walked out into the morning sunshine. He was thinking — 'You can't win them all.'

Bo Higgins was leaning against a hitch rail, stroking his black beard. Trace went toward the kid and beckoned to him. Higgins approached eagerly.

'You're hired, Bo,' Trace told the young man. 'As a civilian associate. I won't deputize you, and you'll be free to put in a claim for any rewards should that come up. Is that all right with you?'

'It's everything I wanted,' Bo Higgins replied. 'Where do you want me to start, Marshal?'

'I think it's best if you start out

drinking in the saloons. You won't have to make up a story for anyone, just tell them the truth that you've been working on the riverboats and got tired of the life. In the meantime, you know how men talk, listen to see if anyone is commenting on strangers in town. Keep your eyes open. You said you saw a wanted poster on Frank Corbett. An illustrated poster?'

'Someone had sketched out his face. I'd know him if I saw him.'

'The Aristas themselves — Regal and Arturo — shouldn't be hard to spot with their Spanish dress and Spanish ways. If you like I can give you a short description of the others back in my hotel room. It might help. I've collected bulletins on every one of them — except the Indian, no one knows what he looks like or even what name he goes by.'

'Regal Arista's slave, you mean.'

Trace was caught short. 'His slave? I was told he was Regal's loyal body-guard because of something Regal once did for him, saved his life maybe.'

'Yeah?' Bo answered. 'That could be it. You know how people like to talk about outlaws. I heard that this Indian was Regal's slave, sold to him by the Indian's own tribe down in Mexico.'

'Anything could be,' Trace admitted, but he eyed Bo Higgins, assessing him. There was no measuring the young, bearded man's guile or lack thereof. It didn't matter. Bo Higgins was the only man he had to work with or was likely to find. Even if Bo's only intention was to garner reward money for himself, he could prove useful.

Returning to his hotel room, Trace named and commented on all of the gang members he knew of, and wrote down brief descriptions of them — Raven and Woody Price included. He then dispatched Bo on his tour of Sheffield saloons while Trace went out to find Sally Cason.

He expected to find her in the little dining room of the hotel, and started that way. On the stairs leading up to the second floor landing he nearly walked into Garret Black. Black was the sort of man you recognize easily, even if like Trace Cavanaugh you had never seen the man in person before.

What Garret Black was was a mean man without concern for, or respect for, any other living thing. Tiny black eyes shining out of a puffed, scowling face reflected belligerence and an anger against the world which had produced such an ugly specimen. In those eyes was only animal brutality without intelligence.

He was barrel-chested, long in the arms. He bulled his way past Trace, bumping shoulders with him. Garret Black was the sort of man who encourages confrontation. That was probably all he enjoyed in life.

Trace hesitated fractionally. With a few quick strides he could drop the barrel of his Colt on to Garret Black's skull. But to what purpose?

Black could be locked up in Marshal Dandridge's flimsy jail cell, but they would get nothing out of him. He would never tell what he knew of Arista's plans without the application of hot coals to the soles of his feet, maybe not even then. Black's arrest would only alert Arista to possible trouble. Trace just noted which hotel room Black entered and continued his way downstairs.

Entering the small, bright hotel restaurant, Trace looked around and finally saw Sally. He had glanced at her twice before the realization of who she was finally settled on him. Trace had given her a few dollars for a dress to replace the singed, filthy one she had been wearing, and she had spent the money well.

Sally Cason was wearing a white dress with tiny flowers embroidered on it — blue, yellow and pink ones. Her hair had been washed, combed and pinned up on top of her small, neat skull. She flashed a welcoming smile at him as he approached the round table where she sat lingering over tea.

'How did it go?' Sally asked.

'Not too well, I'm afraid. Bo's going to continue to be my only help.' He leaned back in his chair, beckoning to the waitress, miming a request for coffee. 'It looks like you had a more fruitful morning.'

'Do you like it?' Sally asked bashfully, looking down at the dress and smoothing it across her lap.

'Very pretty,' Trace said as the waitress returned with a quart pot of coffee and a cup. 'I like your hair too.'

'I had some help with it,' Sally told him. 'A girl from the hotel trimmed off the singed pieces and washed and brushed it out.' Shyly, almost with embarrassment, she added, 'I let her talk me into pinning it up.'

'You look grand,' Trace said, pouring a cup of coffee. 'Have you given it any thought?'

'Given what any thought?' Sally asked.

'Going to see your Aunt Sheila. I'll go along with you. We'll explain things as well as we can. If she was nice to you as a kid, she won't deny you now.'

'She was nice to me because of my father,' Sally said.

'You can't know that.'

'It's so.'

'I know that no decent woman would turn you away under the present circumstances.' Trace leaned forward, folding his hands together. 'Look, Sally, something has to be done with you.'

'To get me out of your way, you mean?'

'That's a part of it, but I need to know that you're somewhere safe when the trouble starts. I can't have your welfare on my mind as well. You have to make some kind of arrangements for yourself. And, if as you believe your father will make a break for Sheila's house should he escape from the Aristas, you'll be there.'

'All right,' Sally said with an unexpressed sigh. 'I suppose you're right. I have nowhere else to go. But, Marshal, not everyone is crazy about finding orphans on their doorsteps.'

'But she's family.'

Sally laughed. 'I doubt that from what I remember of Father and Sheila, but I suppose she's the closest thing to family that I have.' She pushed back her chair and rose. 'Let's get going if it has to be that way.'

Trace said, 'First I want to go by the bank and alert them that Arista is in the area, and why. Stay here for a while if you like, or you can go over to the stable to check on our horses. Try to find out where Sheila lives if you can't recall.'

'I remember,' Sally answered. 'Marshal, despite all of my beauty,' she said in a self-deprecatory tone, 'I believe I'd be better served by changing into range clothes. I splurged and also bought a pair of jeans and a shirt with your money.'

'All right, though I was just getting used to seeing you with your hair up.'

Sally shrugged, 'It goes up, it comes down.' There was a foxy little look in her eyes and Trace frowned. The girl couldn't be, shouldn't be, *wasn't* developing a crush on the old codger that he was, was she? Ridiculous, although he was the nearest thing Sally had to a father, a protector just now. A little gruffly he paid the restaurant tab and said his goodbye.

Bo Higgins was seated on a wooden bench in front of the hotel when Trace exited. Hardly a surprise. He jumped eagerly to his feet. His face behind his dark beard was glowing. He fell in behind Trace as the marshal started out toward the town bank.

'You'll never guess who I just saw!' Bo Higgins said, trying to talk and keep up with the marshal at once. 'Garrett Black! He was in the hotel.'

'I saw him too,' Trace Cavanaugh told the young man.

'You did? Then why aren't we going to tackle him?'

'I can't see the value in it right now,' Trace said. They stepped down as they passed an alley and then up again as they walked past a dry goods store. The bank was two blocks further along.

'But, Marshal, there must be a price on Black's head.'

'Possibly,' said Trace, who knew for a certainty that there was a reward posted for Garret Black.

'Then . . . ?' Bo looked bewildered.

'Trying to take him in would raise a ruckus,' Trace told the man. 'We'd never get him to talk without using torture — probably not even then. We'd be alerting Arista that something was up, that someone was aware of his men being around Sheffield. That might cause him to pull off, or worse, to decide to assault the bank with the full force of his men behind him.

'I can't risk that for whatever money might be on Garret Black's head. There's time to take Black later — we know where he is.'

'I guess that makes sense,' Bo replied. 'Still, . . . ' Still he was only in the game for the possibility of earning the rewards the Arista men carried on their heads.

Trace halted in front of the store window. 'Bo, we do things my way or you don't do them at all. Maybe I should have deputized you after all, to make sure you'd do as I asked.'

'I'll do things your way, Marshal,' Bo muttered. He didn't look angry, but just a little disappointed.

They stepped down to cross the next alley. That was when the gunshots rang out. Two men concealed in the deep shadows of the bank alley cut loose with their pistols as Trace and Bo Higgins were crossing. Trace who had been alert to such a possibility hit the ground and rolled aside, drawing his Colt as he went. Bo stood as if transfixed as three more shots sprayed around them, gouging splinters out of the side of the buildings. Trace reached up, hooked Bo's legs behind the knees and dropped him to the ground.

'Get down you damn fool!' Trace triggered off two shots from his revolver in the general direction of the attackers.

'Who is it?' Bo panted. He had his

own pistol ready, lying on his belly, elbows propping him. If there was ever a time for it, this was it: *Shoot first and ask questions later*. Trace saw one of their attackers jump up and heel it toward the far end of the alley, caught one glance at the fleeing gunman's face and sighted in on him. A running man isn't that easy to hit with a handgun, not at any distance, and Trace's shot only tagged the running man high on the hip, and he was able to stagger away and round the corner of the alley.

'One left,' Bo managed to gasp. 'I think he's behind those barrels.'

Trace didn't answer. Bo was too much the talker. This was no time for conversation.

'I think I can get him,' Bo Higgins said. He was staring down his pistol barrel intently. Now he fired three closely spaced shots into the barrels. The heavy .44 slugs penetrated the empty wooden barrels and tagged flesh. A man howled in pain and tried to leap up and follow his companion down the alley.

Trace went to one knee, steadied his aim and triggered off a killing shot. There would be no escape for this one. A split second later Bo fired himself, his shot going high into the air. The lurking gunman pitched forward on his face and skidded to a lifeless halt against the alley floor, his outstretched fingers seeming to still be reaching for his fallen gun.

Rising, Trace walked toward the dead man, his pistol still at the ready. Sometimes dead men weren't as dead as they seemed. Bo Higgins was in the mood for celebration.

'You got him, Marshal. You got him!'

'No, I didn't. I was watching. It was your shot that took him, Bo.'

'Are you sure? I didn't think that — '

'It was your shot,' Trace repeated. They were hovering over the dead man now. A small crowd had gathered at the head of the alley, watching. Bo holstered his pistol and turned the dead man over. He was a nice looking man with a narrow mustache. The suit he was wearing had been an expensive one.

'That's Monte Dixon,' Bo said in elation. 'I know it is! I remember from the description you gave me!'

'It may well be,' answered Trace who had never seen the Arista rider in person.

'He must be worth at least five hundred dollars, maybe more!' Bo said enthusiastically. He acted like they had been thinning out a pack of marauding wolves. Well, maybe they were, in a way. But Bo looked upon every one of them as just a pelt, not as men. 'Think that marshal will pay the bounty, Trace?'

'I don't know how they do these things around here — it may not have ever come up before now.'

'They've got to pony up,' Bo said determinedly.

'I suppose. Why don't you take him over to Marshal Dandridge and discuss it with him?'

Trace was not surprised to see that the town marshal had not arrived although half the town seemed to have. Dandridge's broken leg was an excuse for not doing anything much at all. A narrow, hesitant young man with a badge on his shirt had appeared, pushing his way through the spectators. One of the town's deputies, no doubt.

'Here's a man who will help you,' Trace said, only now holstering his Colt.

'You mean you aren't coming with me?' Bo asked with surprise.

'That's what I mean. I still have to stick to my plan, and my business has nothing to do with bounties.' Trace showed his badge to the uncertain deputy by way of identification and worked his way through the gathered crowd to the main street once again, leaving Bo and the deputy to discuss the dead man who was almost certainly the trigger-happy Arista rider, Monte Dixon. The first man, the one Trace had sent on his way was an unknown, but from his knowledge of the gang's members and the bulletins in his possession, he had to believe that it had been Victor Segundo. He had a flourishing dark mustache and a chin that been split at one time or another.

It seemed that Segundo was not such a bold man when he did not have a machete in hand like he had used on his wife. He would be limping for a long time to come. Trace knew that his bullet had tagged Segundo in the hip.

Sally would be waiting at the stable by now, but Trace was determined to pay a visit to the bank. There was still a knot of men at the head of the alley behind him when Trace reached the door to the Sheffield bank. 'Enos Pettigrew, Owner and Manager' it said on the half-glassed front door in gilt paint.

Enos Pettigrew looked more like his name than any man had the right to. Stuffy, his narrow face decorated with silver-framed pince-nez, his bald head was nearly undecorated. He obviously thought of himself as master of his own small empire; he was probably a difficult man to get a mortgage extension from. Trace had fastened his badge to his once-white shirt before entering. Pettigrew noted it, nodded and led Trace into a back office where the little man in a light brown suit seated himself behind the desk, began drumming his fingers against the wood and gave out with a peremptory, 'Well?'

'Well,' Trace said with a faint smile. 'You are about to have some trouble in your bank.'

'Nonsense, my bank is run — '

'Gun trouble,' Trace interrupted and Pettigrew's self-satisfied smile faded. He told the banker, 'There is a man named Lucas Cason who comes to check on his safety-deposit box once a year, around Christmas.'

Impatiently Pettigrew reacted. 'The name means nothing to me, and if he only visits the bank once a year, as you say, there's no reason that I should remember him. Besides,' he said as if solving matters, 'it is nowhere near Christmas.' The tapping fingers began their ritual again. Pettigrew peered though strong lenses at Trace, his watery blue eyes annoyed.

'He will be a little earlier this year, and when he comes in he will be accompanied by a man named Regal Arista.'

'Arista?' Pettigrew said, suddenly alert. 'You don't mean the killer and bank robber?'

'I do. Mr Pettigrew, those two intend to remove a large quantity of gold from your bank.'

'To hold us up!' Pettigrew stuttered, half rising in his excitement.

'No, sir, the money is in Cason's safe-deposit box. I would like to take up a position in the bank before that happens.'

'And shoot it out with them! In my bank? No, no, no. I won't allow it. Besides, if the gold is in Cason's box, he has every right to take it out.'

149

'He will be taking it out under threat.'

'Even so . . . ' Pettigrew said, faltering again. 'That is more in your line of business or Marshal Dandridge's. Not mine. I won't have my employees and customers placed in danger.'

'That can be managed,' Trace believed. 'But this is the ideal place to capture Regal Arista. He will likely come alone with Cason so as not to draw undue attention. His thoughts will be focused on what they are doing and not — '

'No, sir, no, no!' an increasingly frantic Pettigrew said. 'Not here. Not in my bank!'

'It would be in your best interest, sir,' Trace said calmly. 'It might save you a lot of legal trouble.'

'What sort of trouble?' Pettigrew asked shrewdly, his eyes narrowing.

'I believe they call it receiving stolen goods from a criminal enterprise. I'm not sure that's the right term. The state attorney will be happy to explain it to you.'

'Preposterous!' Pettigrew got to his feet. 'I had and have no knowledge of any criminality. As for safety-deposit boxes, they are private to the citizen who uses one, and no one in a bank is ever allowed access to whatever they may contain. Which is precisely why we are able to offer them to our customers.'

'You know, Pettigrew,' Trace said, realizing things had reached a dead end, 'this could still go to shooting. If Regal Arista gets twitchy. If something sets him off. You'd be better off with me on the premises, but I suppose it's up to you.' Trace shrugged and positioned his hat before turning toward the door.

'If you are ready for a vacation, now wouldn't be a bad time to consider taking one.'

8

Sally was at the stable when Trace reached it. She stood outside holding the leads to Trace's gray and her inherited red roan. She was wearing her hair down, tied back with a red ribbon. She had on a new pair of blue jeans and a man's red-checked shirt. She showed no signs of impatience though Trace had left her alone for longer than he had intended.

'What's all the uproar over there?' Sally asked, lifting her chin in the direction of Marshal Dandridge's office.

'Bo Higgins is claiming his first bounty. A couple of Arista men tried to bushwhack us in an alley. Bo got one of them; the other ran off.'

'You don't look very happy about it,' Sally said. Trace looked up from what he was doing — double checking his saddle cinches.

'I'm not. All it does is draw attention to us. Let's ride while we talk,' Trace said, swinging aboard his horse.

They passed out of town and found a country lane running through fields where blue and white lupins flourished among the scattered poplar trees. A flock of crows rose from one of these trees and circled, cawing raucously and uselessly.

Sally hesitated and then asked, 'But, if these men were attacking you and Bo shot one, he deserves a reward, doesn't he? And there's one less of the Arista gang for you to worry about.'

'I don't begrudge Bo the bounty. I had just hoped to keep my presence in town a secret for awhile longer.'

'But the ambushers must have already known,' Sally commented.

'They knew. How they knew, I'm not sure. Either Garret Black is not as stupid as he seems to be — ' Trace described his meeting with the thug in the hotel, 'or our old trail friends Raven and Woody Price found Arista and are

153

doing some talking.'

'I can see Raven doing that. It would give him a chance to ingratiate himself with Arista. 'But . . . '

'But, what?' Trace asked, knowing that the girl had more on her mind.

'But Woody would never do that,' she said with an almost anguished expression. 'He liked you, Marshal! And he . . . '

'He liked you as well,' Trace suggested.

'At least well enough that he wouldn't want to place me in harm's way,' Sally finished primly.

They had halted at a rise in the trail. Looking down, Trace could see a small white cottage set amid green grass and sturdy cottonwood trees. It was a cosy-appearing place. Trace glanced at Sally. The girl was looking down, not at the house, but at nothing. Her eyes were damp.

'Is that your Aunt Sheila's place?' Trace asked.

'Yes, it is. Seeing it again brought

back thoughts of Christmas and of Father. I'm not crying!' she blurted out. After a moment she sniffled and added, 'It seems smaller than I remember it.'

'They always do,' Trace said. 'Come on, let's get down there. There's a woman working in a garden beside the house.' He pointed. The woman wearing a blue dress and white sun bonnet was at the side of the house, some sort of vegetables bunched in her hand. She had looked up and now stood watching, hands on hips, as Trace led the way down the trail toward her.

'Is that Aunt Sheila?' Trace asked.

'It's hard to tell at this distance with the bonnet shading her face,' Sally said, squinting that way into the bright sunlight, 'but, yes. Yes that's her.'

As they drew nearer two brown-spotted white dogs ran forward and began circling and yapping. They were young, hardly menacing, just showing some exuberance in welcoming strangers. Entering the tree-shaded yard, Trace saw the woman bundle a bunch of beets in her apron and walk forward. She was older than Trace had expected, though why this should be so if she were Luke Cason's sister, or as Sally obviously suspected, his lover, Trace could not have said.

Of middle years she had a fine facial bone structure. Her hair he saw as Sheila removed her bonnet, was blonde, but there were silver threads running through it. She was trim and small. Her face puckered in puzzlement. She smiled, then seemed to try to conceal the smile. Then she smiled again. The beets fell free as she rushed toward Sally.

'Sally! It is you, isn't it? You've grown so since I last saw you. Step down — both of you,' she said, casting appraising green eyes on Trace, ' — and do come in out of this sun. Things are fine around here in the early morning hours, but . . . '

She chatted on rapidly as people who are long alone and isolated can. She seemed genuinely happy to see Sally, and that was the important thing to Trace. He stepped heavily from the saddle and asked where they could water the horses.

'There's a pump and trough in back of the house,' Sheila told him. 'It's shady back there. You can picket your horses if you've a mind to.'

Trace took the reins to Sally's red roan from her and walked both horses to the rear of the house. He pumped water into the trough and watched as they dipped their muzzles in the cool water. He did not expect to remain long himself, so when the horses had had their fill, he looped the gray's reins loosely over and around a low cottonwood branch. Unsure of what Sally would decide, he tied the roan similarly and made his way back to the front of the house.

The house had a screen porch door, Trace noticed. Quite a modern addition. Behind it the heavy outer door stood open to the scant morning breeze. Trace knocked on the door frame.

'All right to come in?' he called.

'Come along in,' Sheila called from somewhere within the house.

Scraping his boots as best he could, Trace crossed the threshold to find Sally sitting on an overstuffed, plush red sofa, a glass of lemonade between her hands. Her eyes had an uncertain aspect to them. Sheila, leaning against the wall beside the cold fireplace, had an almost smug expression.

The man standing in the interior doorway with the gun in his hand had no expression in his eyes at all. 'Drop your gunbelt, Marshal, or I'll be forced to shoot you.' Trace did not hesitate to comply. The muzzle of the man's blue steel Colt .44 was unblinking, unwavering.

'Luke Cason?'

'That's right,' Cason affirmed, as Trace's gun and belt hit the floor. 'Want to pick that up for me, Sheila?' Cason himself held his position, in the hallway door.

'How'd you get free, Cason? Or did

you just rejoin the Aristas yourself?'

'I got free, that's all,' Cason said with an even savagery. Yes, Trace thought, Sally's father could be a dangerous man if pressed.

'Father, please!' Sally's voice was strained. The lemonade glass was shaking in her hands. 'Marshal Cavanaugh has been a real friend to me, my protector while we were on the trail. He brought me here only to make sure I was safe. Put the gun down!'

'I can't do that.' Luke Cason said. 'I know who Cavanaugh is. Raven was telling us all about him.'

Sally's voice rose to a shriek, 'Raven! How could anybody take his word for anything. Did he tell you about attacking me up along the river?'

'Raven?' Cason said dully. It was obvious he was not fond of the Arista man he must have once known better than any of them, still he was ready to stand for the worst of his former gang members. The way these hoodlums stuck together was almost tribal. 'No,

Raven didn't say anything like that.'

'Did you talk to Woody Price?' A sudden thought occurred to her, 'Woody is all right, isn't he?'

'The blond kid who was riding with Raven?'

'That's the one. Was he . . . ?'

'He was fine the last time I saw him,' Luke Cason replied a little tightly. He returned his steady gaze to Trace Cavanaugh. 'You really have stirred things up, haven't you, Marshal?'

'If you say so,' Trace replied, not wanting to rile Cason who was as taut as new wire already.

'Raven told us how you recognized Bob Shelby on the trail and gunned him down before he had a chance to surrender.'

'That was a lie!' Sally said defensively. 'It was Raven who killed the man.'

'Too bad,' was all Luke Cason said. 'I always sort of liked Bob.' After a moment's silence Luke suddenly blurted out, 'How'd you manage to avoid Victor Segundo and Monte Dixon? I know that Regal sent them into town last night to take care of you.'

'We didn't exactly avoid them,' Trace said, 'just what they had in mind for us. Monte Dixon was always a sudden man with a gun, but he was never much good with one. Victor Segundo is at his best with a machete and facing women. They didn't do their job real well.'

'You shot them both?' Luke Cason asked in disbelief.

'Me and one of my deputies,' Trace said to give Cason something to think about. Sally blinked in surprise, but she said nothing. 'Monte Dixon won't be going back to the outlaw camp. Victor Segundo is alive, but carrying some lead in his hip. I doubt he'll ever be able to mount a horse again without help.'

'Yes, sir,' Luke Cason repeated, 'you really have things stirred things up, Marshal Cavanaugh.'

'I have a job to do, Cason. This is something you seem to have forgotten again — there is such a thing as the good guys and the bad guys.'

'And you're a good guy?' Cason said with a dry, incomplete laugh.

'That's what the law says.'

Sheila had not spoken, had barely moved during the exchange. Apparently she did not believe in interfering in her man's business affairs, whatever they might be.

'That only leaves . . . ' Cason was apparently totaling the dead and wounded on the Arista side.

'Don't count on Garret Black,' Trace said. 'I've seen him, so have a few of my deputies, and some of them are real eager to collect his scalp.' That was almost true — Bo Higgins was not beyond bracing the man in Trace's absence now that the kid had the smell of money in his nostrils.

'Bo . . . ?' Sally said very hesitantly. Trace cut her off.

'Don't mention anyone's name, Sally. Please?'

'I know. You've warned me about that before.'

'What do you think Arista has in mind now, Cason?' Trace asked. 'And, come to that — what do you have in mind? Seems to me you're just running wild. Where did it all start to go wrong?'

For the first time Luke Cason looked tired, looked his age. He lowered the pistol he was holding and slipped it into his holster.

'Do you want to know, Marshal? Would you really like me to tell you exactly what happened?'

'I would much appreciate it,' Trace replied soberly.

Sally, who had never been told about her father's past, leaned forward intently. Sheila, who apparently knew all things, went away softly toward the kitchen. 'Do you mind if we sit down and talk?' Luke Cason asked, removing his hat to wipe his hair back with his hand.

Trace thought it was a better idea than standing up with Cason's pistol trained on his belly. He nodded. Sally scooted along the couch so that her father could sit beside her. Trace took a facing wooden chair with a leather back and seat. Holding his own hat in his hands, he waited. Cason began very slowly; it was as if he were sorting his thoughts out, now and then glancing at Sally as if disliking the possibility that he might diminish himself in her eyes. With a heartfelt sigh, Cason finally began.

'I was younger than Sally is now, no more than seventeen or so, when I found myself on the wrong side of the law. Another boy and myself — his name doesn't matter now — stole a couple of saddle ponies from a rancher down along the Brazos. Led them right out of their corral and rode them away. It was a lark, nothing more. Except the law didn't look at it that way. We were wanted for horse stealing, which is frowned on all across Texas and especially down in that Brazos country. When we found out we were wanted, we rode, Marshal, we rode hard and long.

'One day about a week later, the other boy's horse broke a leg. We tried riding double, but it was slowing us down. This kid just said, 'Ah, the hell with it. I'm giving myself up. Let 'em hang me, I don't care'. I kept on going — never saw him again, don't know what happened to him.

'About a week later down in Laredo, I met a man who carried two guns and looked tough as nails to me. We got to talking over drinks, and I admitted I was on the run. You might know the name he gave, Marshal. It was John Stoddard.'

Trace nodded. He knew the name. Stoddard was one of the old Arista gang who had been shot dead in the streets of Odessa when the whole town turned against the outlaws.

'Old John advised me that I was crazy trying it on my own when there was easier living to be had, and more security from the law with a gang. He told me that he'd speak to Regal Arista about me and within a day or two, I was riding with the gang. I felt that I no longer had a thing to fear.'

'Why didn't you just turn yourself in like the other boy did?' Sally asked. 'Instead of joining up with a rough bunch like that.'

'Had I, you probably wouldn't have been born, Sally. They didn't hesitate to hang a horse thief then. I wasn't willing to see my life end before my eighteenth birthday.'

'The Bisbee hold-up,' Trace urged. That was where Luke Cason's life began to be of interest to Trace.

Luke nodded and told them, 'That was years later, of course. I was trusted as much as any man in the Aristas by then. We had drifted over into Arizona Territory partly because we had heard that the Texas Rangers were determined to take some extreme measures to get rid of us. Well, we came up on a town called Bisbee which had been nothing much but suddenly was booming because of a huge copper strike. The mines had almost two thousand men working for them.

'Regal, who was always a man to grab any opportunity, did some calculating concerning the size of the payroll those men drew. Then he got to the business of finding out where the biggest mine was and where its business office was located.' Luke paused. He looked toward the kitchen.

'Sheila, my throat's getting dry. Can you bring me a glass of that lemonade too?' He said to Trace, 'I haven't talked so much in a long time.'

Trace nodded his understanding. When the silent, softly moving Sheila had given Luke his drink, glanced at Trace who shook his head negatively, she slipped away again toward the kitchen. Luke Cason continued his tale.

'There wasn't much more to robbing that mine office than walking in and waving our guns around for effect. I wouldn't say they were cowards, but they weren't willing to die for the ore company. We got away clean.'

'With fifty thousand dollars,' Trace

said. Luke dipped his chin.

'With fifty thousand dollars.'

'What next?' Trace nudged. Luke was getting around to the important answers to his questions, but slowly. The dogs in the yard began barking again, and they all looked that way. Luke Cason rose to peer out past the curtain.

'They've got a squirrel up one of the trees,' Luke told them, letting the curtain drop. He returned to his seat beside Sally.

'The fifty thousand?' Trace prodded.

'I'm getting to it,' Luke said, as if he didn't like being pushed. 'I'd been doing a lot of thinking since we got our tails whipped over in Odessa. A lot of men I knew and had been riding with got killed that day.

'There was a man with Arista named Danny Bixby in those days. We got to talking along the trail as men will. We both still had the Odessa massacre in our minds. Men shot up and dying all around us on the street . . . Bixby said after we had made our clean getaway from Bisbee, 'Luke, that was it for me. I've got what I need. Five hundred dollars will fix it for me'.'

'Fix what?'

''Luke, there's a warrant out on me for manslaughter — that's all the paper that's following me. I killed a fellow down in McAllen as I might have told you once. Well, Luke, I met this man not long after that. A lawyer, and a prosperous one. He told me that he could fix any judge in the county for a hundred dollars, any judge in Texas for five-hundred dollars. Just said to come talk to him when I could afford my freedom'.

'It got me to thinking that I could find the man myself,' Cason said, 'and throw the fix in with a judge. I mean, all the law knew about me was that ten years before as a seventeen-year-old kid, I had borrowed a horse. I figured that if Bixby could buy his way out of a manslaughter charge, that my warrant could be fixed. It was worth looking into anyway. I never wanted to face a battle like the one in Odessa again.'

'Seems like it was a smart idea,' Sally piped in.

'It was the *only* idea, Sally. The only thing I could try. It had to be done. You see I had met and married your mother only a few months before. She told me that your arrival was already announcing itself to her. I couldn't stand the thought of her watching me get hanged, or shot down. And I wanted to be around when you were born.

'We still hadn't divided the loot from the Bisbee job when we hit Flagstaff a week or so later. Regal and Arturo wanted to check the town for possibilities. Regal had been thinking about hitting another bank for a time. The boys were pretty grumpy. We had been long on the trail and it was summertime — hot as Hades.

'Everyone wanted to go into town to see how much cold beer they could drink. Regal could see that he was going to have a revolt on his hands if he didn't give in, so he did. Three men were to remain behind to watch the Bisbee gold — three of his most trusted men: Raven, Danny Bixby and me. Regal wanted the Indian to stay, but the man wouldn't leave Regal's side, so he relented and took him along.'

'I heard a man say that the Indian was Regal's slave,' Trace Cavanaugh commented. Sally cocked her head and studied him curiously.

'Yes,' Luke Cason nodded his head, 'I think he was. His people owed Regal some sort of debt and the Indian was put into servitude to pay it off. At least that's the way I heard it, and from what I saw of the way Raven treated him and the absolute submissiveness of the man to Regal's whims, indicated to me that it was a true story. The Indian felt that if he failed Regal Arista, he was failing his tribe.'

'What a brutal life,' Sally said in a low voice.

'With Regal Arista around it was pretty brutal no matter who you were,'

Luke Cason said. 'That's why on that day when Raven, Bixby and I were camped out in the pine forest above Flagstaff, and Bixby turned his eyes toward me and said quietly, 'Now's the chance we've been waiting for', I didn't hesitate. I knew what he meant.

'But something had to be done about Raven. Raven had begun to think of himself as a little prince in Arista's kingdom. At least that's the way he acted.' Luke Cason took in a deep breath and let it out slowly. 'Bixby said he'd take care of Raven, kind of cocky like. He braced the man and found out that Raven was as quick as he thought he was. Bixby dropped to the ground, dead.

'I was already on the move. My horse had been ready for hours. Now as their guns opened up, I bolted for the nag and rode away from there as fast as my spurs could encourage that horse to run.'

'So you made it out of the camp with all of that gold money — where were you headed?' Trace asked.

'Just away — as far away as I could get. I knew what they'd do to me if they caught me — scalp me, shoot me, maybe let Victor Segundo hack me up with that machete of his. I was riding fast and scared.'

'You eventually made Sheffield.'

'I did, and I rented a safety deposit box. I was shaking and sweating the whole time, but the banker didn't seem to notice. I took enough money with me to buy those scant acres I was living on. I knew that I was far away from everyone. I guess I also knew that they would come one day.'

'Why did it take them so long to find you?' Sally asked. She had been silent for long minutes, listening incredulously to the tale of her father's early days.

'The way I heard it was that Regal Arista was serving time in the Arizona Territory prison — arrested for riding a townsman down with his horse. Marshal?'

173

'I don't know anything about that,' Trace replied. In fact most of what he knew about the gang had been extracted from Raven, not the most reliable of sources.

'Well they kept him there for three years, mostly it seems to try to drag something out of him about the Bisbee robbery. Almost everyone over there and in Texas knew that the Aristas were behind it.

'Trying to get him to talk would be like trying to open a coconut with a pen knife. You think that Regal Arista would admit to the crime, convict himself, accept a long sentence and hand over fifty thousand dollars he counted as his?'

'No,' Trace answered. 'The question is, why didn't you turn the money in and go ahead with your plan of hiring a lawyer to try to get your youthful crime expunged?'

Luke looked up from the floor. He was being slightly evasive, Trace thought. When Luke answered, it was in slow, measured tones. 'If I'd admitted to having the money and had to go to court, they'd want to know where I got it. It would come out eventually — they could find people who knew that I had ridden with the Aristas. I just decided to wait until things cooled down . . . and,' Luke added as if it had just occurred to him, 'I had a daughter to care for. Her mother had died while I was off . . . doing what I did. I had a piece of land, I was thinking of building a house there. The girl would be raised in poor, lonely circumstances, but she would be with her father. And I would be with her.

'After a while I was sort of able to even forget about the money. I paid my safety deposit box rental by the year and only visited it so that Sally could have a Christmas, since she had so little else way out there where we were living.'

Sheila had emerged from the kitchen to stand against an opposite wall, arms folded, half-smiling. She was in love with the man; that was obvious. And frightened for him.

Trace wondered who had put up the money for Sheila's cottage; he thought he could guess. Luke Cason was telling the truth about most things, it seemed, but he had polished his tale over the years, and maybe the way he told it now in front of his daughter and Sheila Warner wasn't all of it. It didn't matter much to Trace — he still had a lot of work to do, and only Bo Higgins was holding the fort in Sheffield.

And if anything was certain, it was that Regal Arista and his men would descend upon the town. Regal would have that money one way or the other.

'How'd you get away from Arista this time?' Trace asked Luke Cason.

'Art — Arturo Arista — was the only one guarding me last night. When he fell asleep I thumped him, hard, on the skull with the butt of my rifle. I don't think it was enough to kill him, but he's going to have the world's worst headache today. Then I lit out, and there was only one place I would go. One place I would be safe and that Arista knows nothing about.' He glanced at Sheila Warner, with apparent gratitude in his eyes.

'All right,' Trace Cavanaugh said, getting to his feet. 'Let's go, Cason.'

'You're arresting me?' he asked and Trace saw both Sally and Sheila tense.

'I have no warrant on you,' Trace said. 'What might happen to you later is far beyond my control, but no, I'm not arresting you. Have you still got that key around your neck? Good, because we're going into Sheffield to take that money out of the bank before Regal Arista can do it — and he will be coming for the gold.'

9

Luke Cason's horse was beat-down from his hard night ride and so the outlaw was given Sally's fresher red roan. Cason recognized the pony. 'Why, isn't this Bob Shelby's horse?'

'It was. Raven got it for Sally so that he wouldn't have to ride double.'

'By gunning down Bob?'

'I think we already told you that. He had a tale about Bob trying to kill him, but I didn't much believe him. You knew them both, Luke, what do you think?'

'I think what I always have thought: Raven is a damned liar, and a man to mark when he has a gun in his hand.' Cason swung aboard the roan and said nothing more as they trailed out of the yard, Sally standing on the porch of the house with Sheila's arm across her shoulders. Their eyes were watchful, hopeful.

'You really haven't done right by either one of them,' Trace couldn't keep himself from commenting.

'I tried. A man tries, but sometimes you get the wrong result, Marshal.'

Yes, Trace had to admit to himself, that was true: a man tries. It seemed to Trace, however, that a man can only be judged by the stance he takes. And he reflected that if he had not been bullied into make certain choices by wiser heads when he was younger, he could very easily be in Luke Cason's boots right now.

Or worse off.

'What are you going to do with the gold, Marshal, if we get it?'

'I'll have it freighted to my office in Austin. They will contact Bisbee and see what arrangements Arizona wants to make for its return. Luke, I know you still have the key; you haven't forgotten the box number have you?'

'I couldn't. It's the day and month Sally was born. A man doesn't forget important numbers.'

Trace only nodded. Luke Cason's eyes were on the road ahead. As they passed the crows, the lupins and the stand of poplar trees again, Trace decided that Cason was at least being honest about that. The man had tried to go straight since the girl had come to live with him. Even though they were living on stolen money.

'There's someone following us, Marshal.'

'I know. I saw him.'

'What are we going to do about it?'

'Nothing. We're going where he wants us to go, and you're staying alive as long as you're the only one who knows the box number.'

'I'd like to at least know which one it is,' Cason muttered.

'Raven, Regal, Arturo, Garret Black, Frank Corbett, the Indian — take your pick; it's of no real importance right now.'

'Regal never rides alone, nor does the Indian — they're always together. You told me that Victor Segundo was not going to be riding anytime soon with your lead in his hip. Garret Black is so stupid, he'd probably ride up to us and demand my key. I think it has to be Raven, Marshal.'

'Maybe,' Trace said. Conjecture was pointless.

He wondered if Bo Higgins was handy. On this day they would doubtlessly be forced to face what remained of the Arista gang. Was there any point in going back to visit Marshal Dandridge to ask for help? Probably not, he decided. They were only three against the gang — and unfortunately the motives of Cason and Bo Higgins were both suspect. Would they fight for the gold, or take any opportunity to seize it for themselves?

Trace didn't know. He decided that his life was a hell of a way to live, that he was again taking a hand in a rigged game. Everyone had cards showing, but every man of them had a hole card he was not revealing.

The rider who had been trailing them

was now gone. Both men had noticed it, but neither said anything more about it.

Sheffield appeared before them now. The Pecos River, running like silver mercury glittered in the light. They made their way down the hillslope carefully, grim expressions on their faces.

Cason did ask once, 'How are you fixed for ammunition, Marshal?'

Trace figured that was the least of his worries.

Still with no exact plan they rode into Sheffield in the slanting afternoon sun via the western road.

'The bank'll still be open,' Cason commented, as if it were a matter of indifference to him. Maybe it was; his plan had been disintegrating in front of him like a sand castle for a long time. When Trace did not answer, Luke Cason noted, 'I see you're wearing your badge — well, no sense in trying to keep your head down now, is there?'

'No.' Their horses plodded side by

side along the rutted, dusty street. They were three blocks from the bank, one away from the town marshal's office. Trace didn't see any reason to try dragging Marshal Dandridge into things at this point. The shadows in the alleys they passed were deep, the streets only lightly populated. Trace caught no glimpse of watching men in the alleys, at windows, on the roofs of the buildings. Maybe Regal Arista had delayed his plans. He wished he at least had Bo Higgins beside him, but there was no time to go around tracking down the young bearded man. No, he would have to play this out on his own — a deadly sort of solitaire.

Cason was wearing his sidearm. He rode just slightly ahead of Trace. Now Cavanaugh warned him, 'If you try anything at all, Luke, I'll gun you down. You'll never have that money and you'll never see Sheila and Sally again. If you — '

'Save your words, Cavanaugh,' Cason snapped. 'If I was going to cross you I'd have made my try along the trail. I'm sticking with you; I value my life and my freedom more than that gold.'

Trace nodded slightly. Still he saw no sign of any of the Aristas, but they were here, damnit; he knew they were here. The outlaws were not about to ride off and abandon $50,000 or forget the revenge they had planned for Luke Cason. *And* whatever they had planned for Trace Cavanaugh without whom their little plan might have worked out smoothly.

Regal Arista was not the kind to ride away from the money because there would be a fight for it. Raven was not the sort to miss his main chance. Arturo Arista owed Cason payback for what had been done to him during Cason's escape. Victor Segundo, if he were able to ride, must be sharpening his machete to use on Trace for shooting his hip, possibly crippling him for life. The Indian, slave or free man would be wherever Regal Arista was, protecting his master. Frank Corbett was around, and he would be here simply because he loved violence and had now been given a target. Woody Price? Trace had no idea. He hoped that the kid had just decided to run away somewhere.

For Sally's sake, Trace was thinking. He did not want to be the one to gun down Woody who had meant a lot to Sally once.

Their horses were now only a few walking strides from the bank. Luke Cason glanced at Trace. 'Are we ready, Marshal?'

'No, but there's no way to get any more ready.' Trace looked up and down the nearly deserted road through town, hoping for a glimpse of his 'deputy', Bo Higgins, but the bearded kid was not out on the street. They had reached the front of the bank. There was no way of delaying things any longer and no point in doing so. 'We'd better both take our saddle-bags in with us,' Trace said. Cason, still looking weary but calm, just nodded. In his years running with the Arista gang, Cason must have been through tenser moments. The two tramped up on to the wooden porch and entered the bank, saddle-bags over their shoulders.

Enos Pettigrew, the bank manager, stood behind the brass teller's cage, his hands flat on the counter. His face was pallid; he seemed to be trembling. The watery blue eyes behind his spectacles were open wide. In the far corner a young, slender man wearing a red bow tie stood with his hands stiffly at his sides. His face was even paler than Pettigrew's.

'It's only me, Pettigrew,' Trace said. 'No cause for alarm.'

But there was cause for alarm, and Trace knew it instantly. These were not men surprised at the interruption as they went about their daily business; they were scared stiff. Pettigrew's lips moved, but no sound emerged from them. Trace tossed Cason the saddle-bags he had been carrying and said, 'I'll let you get to it, Luke.'

Cason caught the bags and nodded.

But his gun hand had already dropped nearer his holster. Luke was no novice either; the pulse of trouble was strong in the bank. The rifleman appeared suddenly in the back office doorway and levered through two shots, one aimed at each of them. He wore a wide black sombrero with elaborate stitching, black waist-length *vaquero* jacket and flared black trousers. Regal Arista had finally decided to take a hand himself.

Luke Cason was tagged high in the chest as he tried to draw his pistol. Trace had flung himself to the floor of the bank as the shots racketed around the room. He crawled rapidly toward the shelter of the counter behind which Pettigrew had now disappeared, counted to three, then rose up and fired in the direction of Regal Arista. Regal had moved, however. Deeper into the manager's office, or forward on the floor? The counter blocked Trace's view.

There was a silent, deadly pause

which lasted long seconds during which gunsmoke curled toward the low ceiling and flattened, spreading across the bank lobby, and Luke Cason lay writhing on the bank floor.

Where was Regal Arista? And who had he brought with him? Thinking that way, Trace glanced behind him, but no one was approaching the bank's front door despite the roar of the guns. Trace could afford to be patient; Arista could not. The outlaw would have no idea if citizens of Sheffield or the local law, drawn by the gunfire would be rushing even now toward the scene of violence. Trace suspected that most citizens would be scurrying to shelter, and the idea of Marshal Dandridge rushing to the bank on his broken leg was ludicrous.

Arista could not know that, or if he did, impatience drove him to making a rash choice. Beyond the end of the teller's cage there was an open section of counter where depositors or others on bank business could count their money or sign their checks. Regal Arista vaulted the counter there, his rifle held high, his sombrero back on its drawstring. There was a wild, savage gleam in the Spaniard's eyes. He was smiling.

Trace shot him in mid-air.

Arista hit the floor hard, his folded body making a sickening thud as it hit oak planking. He was on his side; his eyes wide open. There was blood in the corner of his mouth. Trace's .44 slug had torn through Arista's throat, leaving no doubt that Arista was dead. His dark blood pooled on the floor and mingled with that of Luke Cason who still lay writhing in pain nearby.

'I'm hit hard, Marshal,' Cason murmured, as Trace scurried that way in a crouch, his eyes flitting from point to point in the smoke-filled room. 'I can still do it, if you'll get me to my feet.'

Trace reached down and with some effort levered Cason to his feet and they started toward the bronze-faced rank of deposit boxes set in the wall. Cason swayed and seemed to be choking on blood, but they reached the boxes.

Behind the counter now Trace could see the pale face and bewildered eyes of Enos Pettigrew peering anxiously at them. Then he saw another man standing in the office door and Trace spun that way, bringing up his Colt.

He was squat and dark as so many Mexican Indians are. There was a rifle in his hands, but he had not shouldered it. He approached three steps and stood looking down at the body of Regal Arista with black, expressionless eyes.

He looked at Trace Cavanaugh and said, 'Thank you, thank you. I am finally free.' Then the Indian turned and snaked away toward the back door of the bank, vanishing like a shadow. The Indian had a deep and troubling tale to tell, Trace was sure, but now was not the time to be wondering about it.

'How're you doing?' he asked, turning to Luke Cason who was bent over toward one of the deposit boxes, barely able to stay on his feet. Blood dripped from his wound on to the bank floor.

'All right — I've got the combination applied. All I need to do is to unlock it with my key.'

The front door to the bank opened, and Trace, expecting anything, turned that way. It was Bo Higgins, gun in hand, his face wearing an expression of concern.

'What's happening here?' Bo asked.

'It's all over — for now.'

Cason had opened the wide, deep safety deposit box, and now Trace joined him in shoveling the collection of gold coins and currency into the pockets of their saddle-bags while Bo stood an uncertain watch. Pettigrew and his clerk still had not emerged from behind the teller's cage.

'We can't carry all of this very far,' Cason panted hoarsely.

No, they couldn't, not just then, the state Cason was in. 'Bo, bring another horse around. Regal's pony should still be out back — have a look.'

Bo scurried out the back door while Trace and Cason finished looting the strongbox of its stolen wealth. When they were finished, Cason looked up with pained eyes. 'I am going to need some help walking,' Cason told Trace. 'I'm sorry.'

'It's all right. I'll have Bo help me get you back over to the hotel; I've still got a room there. Then I'll send Bo off to find a doctor, if they have one in this town.'

'I'll send my teller for Dr Fainer,' Enos Pettigrew volunteered unexpectedly. 'I feel a little guilty about not listening to you in the first place. I'm sorry for that, Marshal. I've got a feeling that if you hadn't been here, these robbers wouldn't have stopped with just that one safety deposit box. They would have gone for our cash drawers and my safe, too.'

The wan but willing teller was sent on his mission after Trace had given the young man his room number at the hotel. Bo Higgins returned to the bank through the back door at the same time as the teller was leaving by the front.

'I've got the three horses out back,' Bo announced. 'I thought you'd rather leave that way. There are a lot of men gathered out front, wondering about the shots.'

'I'll shoo them off,' Pettigrew said. 'I'll need a couple of them to help me clean up, though.' As he said that he stepped from behind the counter and over the still form of Regal Arista.

In a minute they could hear Pettigrew outside, telling the interested onlookers that there was nothing to see, reassuring them that the bank had not been robbed. Trace looked at Bo and said, 'Let's shoulder the bags and help this man to the hotel.'

Outside in the tree-shaded alley, they found Trace's gray, Sally's red roan and a big palomino fitted with an expensive silver-mounted saddle and bossed bridle. Bo told Trace, 'I knew your gray, of course, and the horse Sally was riding. I found this beast back in the trees. He has to have belonged to Arista.'

'Must have,' Trace agreed, noticing the Spanish saddle and the exquisite lines of the golden palomino. Cason was heavy as he sagged his weight against Trace. 'Load up the gold, Bo,' Trace ordered. 'Let's get out of here.'

Trace held Luke Cason upright, debated trying to mount him on Sally's horse and decided not to. They could hobble along as far as the hotel as they were. Getting Cason into the saddle and off again was more effort than it was worth. Bo had thrown one of the heavily laden saddle-bags over the gray and another over the haunches of the big palomino.

'Let's keep that money together, Bo,' Trace said. 'Put both saddle-bags on the gray.'

Bo looked slightly offended, but complied. With Trace clinging to the saddlehorn of the roan and Luke Cason leaning heavily against him, they made their way along the dusty alley to the back door of the hotel. Bo rode the palomino and led Trace's gray horse. He seemed taken with Regal Arista's big gelding. Well, that was all right — let the kid keep him. Bo was flying high now with a $500 reward due to him for the killing of Monte Dixon and with the fallen Spanish outlaw's expensive horse, he was a thousand times better off than when he had arrived in Sheffield on the flatboat. Let him enjoy his moment — for as long as it might last.

Things were still far from certain. How many Arista men were still around? Trace could think of four or five without any consideration. He was nowhere near being home safe with the recovered money.

Struggling through the backdoor of the hotel and up the stairs to Trace's room they met the first of the outlaws who seemed to have them surrounded.

Trace was stumbling along the corridor, the weight of Luke Cason weighing him down. Behind him Bo lumbered with two heavy bags over his shoulders.

Neither was in position for a gunfight when a side door along the hallway opened and the brutish Garret Black stepped out to meet them.

10

'Help you out there?' Garret Black asked with low animal cunning showing in his dark eyes.

Trace halted in his clumsy motion. He had his right arm around the injured Luke Cason. His holster was pinned between them. Bo Higgins was in a little better position, though he was weighted down by the two pairs of heavy saddle-bags. Bo, however was directly behind the marshal and Cason. There was no shot possible.

'Worried about reaching your gun?' said Garret Black, striding forward heavily. The man was a stalking bear. 'Don't worry. I don't think I want to start shooting in the hotel, anyway. I don't need a gun for what I'm about to do to you.'

'Yes you do,' the strange yet familiar voice said from behind Trace. He glanced that way to see Marshal Dandridge behind them. The stumpy marshal leaned on one crutch, but this was on the side opposite his pistol. He took a step forward, his plastered leg swinging heavily. Now, beyond Garret Black, Trace caught sight of another man creeping along the hallway. It was the thinly built deputy Trace had seen before. He looked nervous, but the gun in his hand was not shaking.

'I'm taking you in, Garret,' Dandridge announced.

'The hell you are!' Garret roared. He reached for his own holstered revolver, only in that moment realizing that there was another armed man behind him. He spun that way and Dandridge shot him. At almost the same moment the deputy fired and Garrett sagged heavily to the floor, black acrid gun smoke swirling around the hallway.

Trace glanced at Bo Higgins, inclined his head and they started into Trace's room.

'That was a near thing,' Bo said, dropping the saddle-bags with relief.

'You got cheated out of your bounty for Garret,' Trace said.

'Yes, but we're both alive.'

They got Luke Cason on to the bed. He was still bleeding, but it seemed not so profusely. There was nothing they could do but wait for the doctor.

'Kind of odd, the marshal being here when we needed him,' Bo said. Trace, at the door, keeping watch for the doctor, only nodded.

He had the idea it was not coincidental that Dandridge had arrived just then. The marshal, who had shown no inclination to help Trace before, had shown up immediately after the stolen money had been retrieved from the bank. Probably Enos Pettigrew had told the marshal what had happened.

Beyond Dandridge, his deputy and the dead Garret, Trace saw a fussy little man carrying a black bag arrive in the hotel corridor.

'Howdy, Dr Fainer,' he heard Dandridge say.

Fainer looked at the sprawled figure of Garret Black. 'Is this the man I'm supposed to treat?'

'I think he's a little past that, Doc. Your man's in there,' he said, nodding toward Trace Cavanaugh's room.

Fainer veered that way. 'Gunshot?' he asked Trace and Trace nodded.

'Seems to be a lot of that going around. Almost an epidemic,' the doctor said, going to Luke Cason's bed. The little man chuckled at his own weak joke, but he opened his black bag and got to work on Cason immediately. Trace restrained himself from asking the questions everyone always did — How bad is it? Will he make it? — and let the doctor do his best. He admired doctors. He didn't see how they could carry on day after day among the sick and the wounded.

Marshal Dandridge entered the room, let his eyes flicker to Luke Cason, then told Trace, 'The banker told me what happened. I guess I should have listened to you. Well, you've got your hands full now. Why don't I take the gold over to my office and store it in the safe? It'll be secure there.'

'I guess I'll be keeping it with me.' Trace said and the town marshal's face darkened. 'I thank you for offering. And,' he said lifting his chin, 'for removing Garret Black from my list.'

'If you're sure,' Dandridge said without much approval, 'but I've got a good strong safe.'

'I'm sure you do,' Trace said flatly, 'but I'd hate to have to count the money all over again.'

Dandridge didn't care for the remark, but there was nothing he could say. He went out and they could hear him giving his deputy instructions on having Garret's body removed before they heard him limping away down the corridor on his crutch.

'Didn't trust him?' asked Bo Higgins, who had taken up residence in the wooden chair near the half-open window.

'I'm not letting that money out of my sight, that's all,' Trace said, returning his eyes to the bloody work of the doctor, 'not after what we've gone through to recover it.'

When the doctor had finally finished and washed his hands in the basin, rolling down his sleeves, he told Trace, 'That was a bad wound, but I think he'll be all right — with a lot of rest.'

Trace thanked the doctor, paid him and saw him out the door.

Bo remained where he had been seated, staring out the window at the town and the Pecos River beyond. 'Missing life on the river?' Trace asked, and Higgins laughed.

'No, I can't say that, Marshal. But, there's a lot to be said for the silence and the solitude out there.'

'Marshal?' The voice that spoke was weak and seemed far distant. Trace turned toward it to see Luke Cason, his eyes open but fluttering. The wounded man lifted two fingers, beckoning Trace to his bedside.

'What is it, Cason?'

Cason licked his dry lips. 'I didn't tell you the whole truth of things back there,' he said.

'I never thought you did.'

'No?' Cason hardly looked surprised. 'You are going to take care of Sally and Sheila, aren't you?'

'Yes.' Although Sheila and Sally would never see the sort of money Luke Cason had been amassing for them.

'Well, then . . . ' Cason's eyes closed and he drifted off into a morphine-induced sleep.

'What was he talking about?' Bo Higgins asked as Trace turned away from the sleeping man.

'That? Oh, Cason spun me a neat little tale on how he had come by the money, what he had done afterward and how he had decided to go straight — and still hold on to the money. It didn't hold together. For one thing there were whole years unaccounted for. I suspect that Cason might have been coming and going, building up his small fortune in various ways.' Trace shrugged. 'I didn't try to question him about it — what was the point?' There was no point in it; Cason had apparently adjusted his story so that Sally would not be ashamed of him. His story was a lie, and if questioned further, he would have continued to lie. Trace thought at the time that he would have liked to ask 'Sheila Warner' a few questions, but there was no point in that either — Sally was back where she belonged.

'I have no warrant on him and nothing I can charge him with. Whatever he was up to in those missing years, it looks like he's gotten away with it.'

'You're a forgiving man, Marshal,' Bo commented.

'No, I'm not, but as I said I have no proof, and anyway I have more important things on my mind just now.'

'Where to now?' Bo asked, rising.

'When Cason and I were riding back to Sheffield someone followed us along for a way and then turned back toward Sheila's house. It could have been any of the Aristas, but most of them have been accounted for now. That leaves Raven.'

'You think he's gone to their house?' Bo asked. 'But why?'

'Raven may have been counting cards. The Aristas, one by one, are coming up dead or wounded — or vanished, like the Indian. He might think that I can actually take this hand. He is a cunning man. He may think that I'll bring Cason back and be carrying the money with me. Or if I've stashed it, he will have the two women as hostages to hold for ransom. It's his best chance, alone, to play his cards. And the pot is huge.'

'He doesn't sound like a nice man,' Bo said in understatement.

'No,' Trace admitted, 'but he is clever.'

And how clever had Trace, himself,

been in letting the convict deal him into the game? It had seemed like the right thing to do at the time. Now it looked to be as poor a decision as playing an inside straight.

All that mattered at this point was getting the two women away from Raven, whose history with all members of the opposite sex was dark and unhealthy.

'We're taking the money?' Bo asked, toeing one of the saddle-bags.

'We can't leave it here.'

'All right,' Bo said with a sigh. He rubbed his sore shoulder. 'Let's give it a try, Marshal. I just hope you know what you're doing.'

Trace smiled thinly, picking up one of the bags. 'There's always hope,' he said.

Right now Trace was just playing the cards he had been dealt; there was nothing more he could do.

'We'll use the palomino as a pack horse — if he'll stand for it. Some horses will, some won't. Some won't accept a strange rider, either. We know the roan and my gray won't be balky with us aboard, so let's try to distribute the weight evenly.' The tall palomino was compliant. Bo Higgins stood admiring the animal whose white tail and mane were lifted by the breeze off the river.

'What do you plan on doing with the animal, Marshal?'

'Hadn't thought of it. I've no use for a second horse. Maybe find a man without a horse and give it to him.'

Bo smiled and swung aboard the roan after handing the palomino's lead to Trace. Bo continued to smile as they trailed out toward the east end of town, moving toward Sheila Warner's house. No wonder, Trace thought. In a single day off the river, the bearded young man had made $500 and fallen heir to an extremely valuable horse and outfit.

The landscape, now familiar to Trace rose and fell as the sun began to fade toward evening. Bo Higgins had little to say, and that suited Trace. Raven was at

Sheila's house; he could sense it. How would the convict play his hand? With guile or pure force? With Raven there was no telling, but he was holding the high cards with the two women as hostages. What was the best way to approach this? Try to approach the house unseen, wait until dark, act as if he had no idea that Raven would be there?

Trace decided there was no best way. It just had to be done.

Sometimes you won the hand by the way the cards had been dealt, sometimes by the way you played them. Sometimes just through dumb luck.

From the rise of the trail now they were looking down on the small cottage and surrounding trees. There was no horse to be seen; Raven would have concealed his, probably in the barn.

'Stay ready now, Bo,' Trace cautioned, 'I can't predict how this is going to go.'

'Hell, Marshal, we've been winning up to now.'

'There's always the last hand, Bo. And we're playing against the man with the deuces.'

Bo, who had never been told the story of the four deuces, smiled. Trace frowned. Sometimes he wondered about Bo Higgins. They started down the slant of the road in the gloom and gleam of twilight. There were bright spots of light scattered about among the trees, enough shadow to conceal a man in others. No one emerged from the house to greet them as they rode into the yard.

'He's in there,' Trace said in a muffled voice. He was somehow sure of it. Raven was in there thinking he was now playing the winning hand, probably holding the two women at gunpoint as he waited for the loot to be delivered to the doorstep.

'What's our plan?' Bo Higgins asked as they sat their horses in front of the porch.

'There is none. We just have to take the man down before he can harm the women.'

'It's a gamble,' Bo said. Trace just nodded. It was a large gamble with the fate of two women hanging in the balance. He swung down from the gray's back. All was quiet inside the house. No one had come out to welcome him. No dogs were around barking. The heavy front door was closed, even in this heat, although Sheila had one of those new screen doors. Raven was there, all right.

'Ready, Bo?'

'Hardly, but we might as well get it over with.'

Raven would want to talk for a minute, just to make sure that they had brought the gold. If he had been looking out the window he must have been able to spot Regal Arista's big palomino, but it would not be so easy to ascertain at a distance what it was that the palomino carried.

Trace swung the screen door open. He held his pistol beside his ear, barrel skyward. He glanced once at Bo who also had his revolver drawn and reached for the heavy interior door's knob. The door was unlocked — what would have been the point in locking it? Raven wanted them to come in. Trace nudged the door with his toe and it swung open slowly on oiled hinges.

The two women sat together on the red plush sofa. Sally's entire body was trembling, her eyes wide. Sheila's face was pale, drawn, but she seemed to have herself under control. Behind them with a gun positioned between their two skulls stood Raven, a smile on his lips, his eyes glittering.

'I wasn't sure you could pull it off, boss,' the convict said, 'but I placed my bets on you. That's Regal's horse out there, isn't it?'

'He won't be needing it anymore,' Trace said without lowering his Colt. 'you want to just give it up, Raven, and let me take you back to the prison.'

'I never thought of you as a funny man, boss, but that is funny. I'm not throwing my cards in now.' He nudged the muzzle of his pistol against Sheila's skull, behind her ear.

'You're still showing a lot of your body as a target,' Trace said.

'You won't shoot. You know how long it would take for my finger to twitch and remove this lady from the planet.'

Sheila spoke up, but not to plead for her life. She wasn't that kind of woman. 'How's Luke, Marshal?'

'He got shot, but the doctor has come and gone. He says Luke will be fine.'

'Thank God,' Sally murmured. She had not stopped trembling yet.

'You can catch up on that later. Marshal, I want your boy here,' he said, meaning Bo, 'to drop his gun and leave the house.' Raven paused. 'Why does he look familiar? Without the beard . . . never mind.'

'I'm not sending him out, Raven. I prefer the odds this way.'

'Do you?' Raven grinned, flashing his white teeth. 'Boss, I'm not alone either.'

'There's another man,' Sheila blurted out. 'Hiding in the kitchen.'

'As Trace watched, the blond kid, Woody Price, moved into the room, holding his own pistol in his rigid hand.

'I was hoping your road had turned in another direction,' Trace said to Woody.

'I just came along to see Sally,' Woody said. 'I don't want any of that damned money.'

Trace saw Raven frown. As Woody stepped nearer, Trace could see that the kid's gun was trained on Raven. Raven spun that way as Bo Higgins shouted out, 'I'm with you, Raven!'

Trace had the moment he had been waiting for. As Raven turned away from Sheila and Sally, he crouched and fired a .44 slug into the outlaw's body. Raven turned back, snarled and folded to the floor.

'Watch it, boss!' Woody Price yelled, and before Trace could respond, Bo Higgins fired, his bullet spinning past Trace's head to thud into the wall. Woody's gun spoke almost simultaneously, and a slug from his Colt

213

caught Bo in the chest. The bearded man flung out his arms and staggered backward, falling through the open door, taking the screen with him.

Rising to his feet as the dark gunsmoke clogged the room, Trace saw that Woody Price had already flung his pistol aside and was now sitting on the sofa beside Sally, his arm around her, Sally's face buried against his shoulder.

'Damn,' Sheila said, lifting herself off the couch. 'It took me three months to get one of those newfangled screen doors from St Louis. Anybody want some coffee?'

Trace made sure that there was no life left in Raven nor in Bo Higgins. He was remembering a few things that Bo had said which should have made him wary. Sally was sitting upright now, hands clasped together, her face tear-streaked.

'Who was Bo Higgins?' Trace asked Woody.

'He was Raven's cell mate before I got to prison. Bo was rolling up his mattress prior to being released just as I checked in.'

'He'd heard all of Raven's stories then — about the four deuces, about Luke Cason and the stolen gold, about the Indian being Regal's slave?' Woody, still pale and shaken, nodded. His hand had stretched out stealthily to cover Sally's.

'I suppose he must have over the course of a couple of years. Raven loved to talk about himself. Funny, Raven who had shared a cell with Bo Higgins didn't recognize him beneath that black beard. I knew in a second who he was. Then he yelled out that he was with Raven. I had to shoot him, boss.'

'I know you did. He was trying his best to kill me,' Trace replied. Then, smiling and frowning at once, Trace said, 'It seems that Bo got his wish — he's with Raven now.'

11

Morning was bright and clear, the air as fresh as if it had just rained. The evening before, Trace and Woody had buried the badmen at the rear of the house, far enough away so that their presence could not recall bad memories. They had let the dogs out of the barn where Raven had locked them up and they emerged in a tumbling, writhing tangle of joy then bee-lined it for the house where Sheila was waiting to feed them. The horses were put up and Trace was offered a bed in the house which he declined.

'Uneasy about us, Marshal?' Sheila had asked with a bent little smile.

'No,' Trace assured her, 'but I've made it this far with the money, and I mean to see it safely on its way.'

Woody had accepted the offer of the spare bedroom; Trace made up his bed in the straw in the barn, his Colt not far from his hand, the gold at his feet. In the morning, then, they made their departure for Sheffield. Sheila and Sally were determined to check up on Luke Cason. Woody asked, 'Are you sure you want me along, boss?'

'Grab your pony,' Trace said sternly. 'You're still under arrest, you know?'

The two women rode ahead of them as they crossed the highlands. They were eager to see Luke. Woody and Trace hung back a little. They spoke as they rode, Trace leading the big palomino and its burden of gold.

'Still puzzles me how Bo Higgins came to be here,' Woody commented. Trace told him about the passage downriver he and Sally made together.

'Higgins was listening to every word Sally said, and he managed to put it all together once she mentioned her name and the name 'Raven'. Bo had heard all about the copper mine robbery and Cason's treachery from Raven when they were cell mates.'

'I guess old Bo wasn't so dumb,' Woody said. Then he realized where Bo Higgins was this morning and just shook his head.

'No. Raven wasn't dumb either,' Trace replied. 'The thing is, Bo Higgins wasn't smart enough to see that he had it made now. He had five hundred dollars in reward money coming to him, and that big animal,' he gestured toward Regal Arista's palomino. 'A lot of men would see that as a fortune and a start on a new life.'

After a mile when they again passed through the poplar trees, and again startled the crows who lived there into flight, Woody found the courage to ask, 'What about me, boss?'

'What do you mean?' Trace asked.

'I mean . . . am I going back to prison?'

'I don't think so — I can't see that doing the state any service. You'll need to help out Sheila and Sally for a while, until Luke gets back on his feet. You'd better stay around here.' Trace paused.

He had been thinking about Woody for some time. 'I believe that you and Raven were both killed fighting the Arista gang. I'll put in for posthumous pardons for you. There won't be any fuss about that. It's only a matter of some paperwork.'

The tightness in Woody's shoulders and back relaxed and he sat his horse less woodenly as they approached Sheffield.

'There's still a few of the Aristas scattered about,' Woody said as they started down the slope toward town.

'I know.' Trace answered. 'Let's see — there's Victor Segundo with a bullet in his hip that will probably cripple him for life. There's Frank Corbett who made his reputation with a knife, not with a gun, and there's Arturo Arista. That's not really a threatening bunch, is it?

'I suppose that Arturo — if Luke didn't crack his skull harder than he thought — might try building a new gang, but he hasn't his brother's magnetism, and the gang hasn't fared too well of late. I think the Aristas are dead as an organization. Which is what my mandate was when I started this way.'

'That and the stolen money,' Woody reminded Trace.

'Yes, and we're going to finish up with that right now. Head over toward the freight yard, I want to talk to the boss about shipping the money to Austin.'

The two women rode on ahead, Sally looking back their way with concern. Woody himself appeared worried still as Trace met with the freight officer who gave him assurances about shipping that much cash money. 'We're insured up to half a million dollars for any loss,' he told Trace.

Trace signed a few documents, then the two shook hands and went out to the horses. The palomino was led around to the back yard of the freight office where two men with shotguns and dour expressions stood watch. The gold was shifted from the back of the palomino to a freight company strong-box, and then it was done. All that was left for Trace to do was to send a wire to Austin, telling them briefly what he had done and that the Bisbee hold-up money was on its way.

Trace saw a kid of ten or twelve perched on the top rail of the pole corral, his eyes wide with astonishment as the big palomino with its flowing white mane and tail was led past him, the silver ornaments on its saddle and bridle gleaming in the sun. Two men standing by only glanced up. They were regular yard hands, apparently.

'Give me a minute,' Trace said to Woody.

'I've got time. I'm dead, am I not?' Woody asked with a grin. He sat his horse patiently as Trace led the palomino toward the kid on the fence.

'You ever see anything like this horse?' Trace asked the kid, who was too dumbstruck to answer now that the palomino was close to him. 'Neither have I. You see this badge I'm wearing?'

The kid nodded his head vigorously though his face was uncertain.

'This is my horse. Anyone asks, you tell them a state marshal said it was all right.' He handed up the reins to the kid, whose dark eyes had opened to the size of saucers.

'What do you . . . ?' the kid asked falteringly.

'I mean that the horse is yours. All legal. Take him home, son.'

One of the two yard workers who had been nearby turned a stunned expression toward Trace as the kid instantly slid from the rail on to the palomino's back and was now racing toward home on it, his face wild with glee.

'Mister,' the yardman asked, 'have you any idea what a horse like that, outfitted like it is, is worth?'

'Yes,' Trace answered, watching the kid ride free on the palomino, whooping to the skies, 'but there's no amount of money worth more than that.'

Woody, who had been waiting patiently,

hands crossed on his pommel, grinned as Trace returned on his gray.

Trace spoke before Woody could say a word. 'What do I need with another horse?'

'You are a puzzle,' Woody said, turning his horse toward the street.

'Most men are,' Trace answered. 'Get over and see to those women. They'll be needing your help for a while.'

'Yes, sir,' Woody answered. 'I will do that.'

'And Woody,' Trace said warningly, 'I don't ever want to see you again.'

'Boss,' Woody Price said with a grin, 'those are the finest words of farewell ever spoken.'

THE END

We do hope that you have enjoyed reading this large print book.

Did you know that all of our titles are available for purchase?

We publish a wide range of high quality large print books including:
Romances, Mysteries, Classics
General Fiction
Non Fiction and Westerns

Special interest titles available in large print are:
The Little Oxford Dictionary
Music Book, Song Book
Hymn Book, Service Book

Also available from us courtesy of Oxford University Press:
Young Readers' Dictionary
(large print edition)
Young Readers' Thesaurus
(large print edition)

For further information or a free brochure, please contact us at:
Ulverscroft Large Print Books Ltd.,
The Green, Bradgate Road, Anstey,
Leicester, LE7 7FU, England.
Tel: (00 44) **0116 236 4325**
Fax: (00 44) **0116 234 0205**

POWDER RIVER

Jack Edwardes

As the State Governor's lawmen spread throughout Wyoming, the days of the bounty hunter are coming to a close. For hired gun Brad Thornton, this spells the end of an era. The men in badges aren't yet everywhere, though, and rancher Moreton Frewen needs immediate action: rustlers are stealing his stock, and Thornton is just the man to make the culprits pay. But these are no run-of-the-mill cattle thieves. The Morgan gang are ruthless killers, prepared to turn their hands to anything from bank robbery to murder . . .

THE HONOUR OF THE BADGE

Scott Connor

US Marshal Stewart Montague was a respected mentor to young Deputy Lincoln Hawk, guiding his first steps as a lawman and impressing upon him the importance of the honour of the badge. Twenty years later, the pair are pursuing a gang of bandits when Montague goes missing, presumed murdered. For six months, Hawk continues the mission alone, without success. But when he stumbles into the gang's hideout, there is a great shock in store. Seems his old companion isn't six feet under after all . . .